DOCTOR WHO AND THE
ROBOTS OF DEATH

DOCTOR WHO
AND THE
ROBOTS OF DEATH

Based on the BBC television serial *The Robots of Death*
by Chris Boucher by arrangement with the British
Broadcasting Corporation

TERRANCE DICKS

A TARGET BOOK
published by
the Paperback Division of
W. H. ALLEN & CO. LTD

A Target Book
Published in 1979
by the Paperback Division of W. H. Allen & Co. Ltd
A Howard & Wyndham Company
44 Hill Street, London W1X 8LB

Printed in Great Britain by
Richard Clay (The Chaucer Press) Ltd, Bungay, Suffolk

ISBN 0 426 20061 6

Contents

1

Sandminer

Like a city on the move, the Sandminer glided across the desert sands.

Not quite a city, a mobile factory perhaps. There were storage holds, control rooms, laboratories, living quarters, food stocks, a recycling plant . . . The Sandminer was completely self-contained, able to range the deserts for years at a time before returning to base. Powered by its mighty hovercraft mechanisms, the Sandminer glided over the fine shifting sands, a massive metal crab on an immense, multi-coloured sea of sand.

It was about to become a ship of death.

Inside the Sandminer robots were everywhere. They stalked silently through the long metal corridors on mysterious errands, they laboured in the engine-rooms and the storage hoppers, they worked on the vast, complex control-deck.

There were three kinds of robot. Simplest and most numerous were the D class, or Dums, programmed to obey orders and carry out simple repetitive tasks. The more sophisticated Vocs could not only obey but respond with speech as well, and even exercise a certain limited independence. Finally there were Super-Vocs, robot commanders, to control their fellows, passing on the

7

orders of the human masters.

Robots were manning the control deck now. V.14 stood watching the huge central screen of the radar spectroscope set high in one wall. It was alive with a swirling vortex of colours. V.32 was poised at a nearby control-console.

'Turbulence centre, vector seven,' said V.14. The robot voice was calm, measured, completely emotionless. All the robots sounded very much alike. With practice the human ear could detect the minute differences between one robot voice and another . . . if anyone cared to take the trouble.

'Scan commencing—now,' replied V.32. A complex pattern of radar traces began flowing across the screen.

In the recreation area most of the human crew were resting. What else should they do? All the routine work of the Sandminer was carried out by the robots.

The recreation area formed an astonishing contrast to the rest of the Sandminer. It was softly carpeted, warmly lit, furnished with scattered couches and low tables, ornamented with colourfully glowing tapestries and ornamental statuary.

It was a room for humans.

At this particular moment, the humans in question were off-duty. Luxuriously robed, faces elaborately painted, they were passing time in a variety of ways. Commander Uvanov was playing three-dimensional chess with a Voc-class robot, V.9. Uvanov was older than the others, with a lined, weary face. As if to compensate, his face-patterning was more elaborate, his robes and head-dress even more fashionably ornate than the rest of them. His thin face was decorated with a wispy, pointed beard. He was frowning in ferocious concentration, although he knew that the robot was, by definition, unbeatable. Playing against a

8

robot, the most you could hope for was a draw.

Neat and precise as ever, more soberly dressed than the others, Dask stood watching the game. With quiet satisfaction he saw Uvanov had already lost—he just hadn't realised it yet.

The two female members of the crew sat on adjoining couches. Zilda was studying some charts, her dark-skinned, beautiful face set in a frown of concentration. Toos, equally attractive, older and more sophisticated, lay back nibbling crystallised fruits from a silver box. Cass, young and muscular, dark-skinned like Zilda, sat close to the two women, dividing his attention between them.

Then there was Borg, his burly figure stretched out on a couch while robot V.16 massaged his shoulder with delicate metal fingers. The sly, round-faced Chub sat looking on. As usual, he was passing the time by tormenting Borg. 'There was a robot masseur in Kaldor City once, Borg ... Specially programmed, equipped with vibro-digits, subcutaneous stimulators, the lot. You know what happened?' Chub paused artistically. 'Its first client wanted treatment for a stiff elbow. The robot felt carefully all round the joint, then suddenly, it just twisted his arm off at the shoulder!' Chub chuckled. 'All over in two seconds ...'

Borg scowled. 'I never heard that.'

Chub nodded. 'It happened—in Kaldor City.'

Dask looked up from the chess board. 'What was the reason?'

'Reason? It went haywire! I wouldn't let a robot work on me for all the zelanite in this ship.'

'Shut up, Chub,' growled Borg. But all the same he waved the robot away.

'A Voc-class robot,' said Dask precisely, 'has over a million multi-level constrainers in its control circuitry. *All* of them would have to malfunction before it could perform such an action.'

Toos popped another fruit into her mouth. 'That's your trouble, Dask,' she said indistinctly. 'You take all the magic out of life.'

Chub looked resentfully at Dask. He was spoiling the joke.

'They go wrong, my friend. It's been known.'

Dask shook his head. 'Only when there's an error in programming. Each case on record shows——'

'Well, this was a case! It pulled his arm off!'

Zilda joined in the teasing. 'I heard it was a leg!'

Poul came in, a medium-sized, quietly self-contained man with an air of constant watchfulness. 'We're turning!' he said. 'Anybody noticed?'

No one had, and no one cared. The robots were running the Sandminer. That was what they were for, after all.

V.9 made his final move, springing a long-prepared trap. 'Mate in eight moves, Commander.' There was no trace of triumph in the calm, pleasant voice.

Uvanov threw himself back in his chair in disgust. 'Never!'

'I will check, Commander.' There was a moment's silence. V.9 said placidly, 'Mate in eight moves. The computation is confirmed.'

'Damn!'

Dask smiled. 'They *are* unbeatable,' he said softly.

There was a beep from the communicator at Uvanov's elbow. Glad of the distraction he snarled, 'Yes?'

'V.14 on scanner, Commander,' said a robot voice. 'We have a storm report. Scale three, range ten point five two, timed three zero six. Vector seven one and holding.'

Uvanov leapt to his feet. 'Full crew alert, V.14.'

'Full crew alert, Commander.'

Suddenly the whole place was bustling with movement.

'Chub, break out an instrument pack,' ordered Uvanov. 'The rest of you with me! Let's hope this one's worth chasing!'

10

It was time for work. If their luck held good, a fortune was rushing towards them at a thousand kilometres an hour.

Meanwhile another kind of craft was spinning through the Space Time vortex, simpler in appearance, infinitely more complex in design. From the outside it looked like an old-fashioned blue police box of the kind used for a time on the planet Earth. Inside, it was a Space Time craft known as the TARDIS.

In the control room, which was dominated by a many-sided central control console, a tall shirt-sleeved man with a mop of curly hair was brooding over the controls. Beside him, a girl in a brief costume made of animal skins was making a flat wooden disc climb up and down a length of string.

The girl's name was Leela, and she had just become the Doctor's travelling companion, choosing to leave her own planet and accompany him on his wanderings through Time and Space. She had joined the Doctor in the hope of adventure—and this wasn't what she'd expected. Apart from anything else, her arm was getting tired . . . 'Doctor, can I stop now?'

'What? Well, of course you can if you like.'

'It won't affect all this?' With her free hand Leela gestured around the control room.

'Affect it? It's a yo-yo—a game. I thought you were enjoying it!'

Indignantly Leela tossed the yo-yo aside. 'You said I was to keep it going up and down. I thought it was part of the magic!'

The Doctor frowned reprovingly at her. 'Magic, Leela? Magic?'

Leela sighed. 'I know. There is no such thing as magic.'

'Exactly,' said the Doctor grandly. 'To the rational mind, nothing is inexplicable, only unexplained.'

'Then explain to me how this—TARDIS of yours is larger on the inside than on the outside.'

For a moment the Doctor was taken aback. Far more sophisticated minds than Leela's had been baffled by the Time Lord technology that had produced the TARDIS. 'Well, it's because inside and outside aren't in the same dimension.'

Leela looked blank.

'All right, Leela, I'll show you.' The Doctor rooted inside the storage locker set into the TARDIS console and produced two boxes, one large, one small.

The Doctor held up the boxes, one in each hand. 'Now, which box is larger?'

Leela pointed. 'That one.'

The Doctor nodded, put the smaller box on the console in the forefront of Leela's vision, and carried the larger one to the far side of the control room, holding it up in line with the first. 'Now, which is the larger?'

Leela pointed to the box in the Doctor's hands. 'Still that one.'

'But it *looks* smaller, doesn't it?'

Leela looked. The small box, perched on the console just before her eyes, seemed to loom larger than the more distant box in the Doctor's hands. 'That's only because it's farther away.'

The Doctor came back to her side. 'Exactly! If you could keep that box exactly the same distance away, and have it here . . .' He tapped the box. 'Then the large box would fit inside the small one!' He beamed triumphantly at her.

'That's silly!'

'That's trans-dimensional engineering,' said the Doctor severely. 'A key Time Lord discovery!'

There was a sudden wheezing, groaning sound and the

12

centre column of the control console stopped moving. The Doctor rubbed his hands. 'This is the exciting bit!'

'What is?'

'Seeing what's outside. We've landed, Leela!' The Doctor switched on the scanner. A blank metal surface filled the screen. They could just get a glimpse of a corner and another surface stretching away. 'It's metal,' said the Doctor. 'We've landed inside something metal!'

'How can we?'

The Doctor waved his hands. 'Well,' he said vaguely, 'you know, one box inside the other. I've just explained it to you!'

'Not very clearly!'

'Well, it's a very dull subject,' said the Doctor dismissively. He shrugged into his coat, put on his hat, and began winding an immensely long scarf around his neck. 'I wonder where we are.'

'You mean you don't know?'

'Well, not precisely, no . . .'

'You cannot control this machine?'

'Of course I can control it,' said the Doctor indignantly. An innate streak of honesty forced him to add, 'Nine times out of ten . . .' He considered. 'Well, seven times . . . five times . . . Oh, never mind, let's see where we are.'

He touched a control, and the doors began to open.

Leela snatched up the crossbow she had brought from her native planet. 'You won't need that,' said the Doctor confidently.

'How do you know?'

'I never carry weapons. If people see you mean them no harm, they never hurt you.' The Doctor paused. 'Nine times out of ten,' he added thoughtfully, and went out into the darkness.

Obediently, Leela put down the crossbow, but she stroked the hilt of the knife that nestled reassuringly at her hip. Leela had been brought up as a warrior in a time of

13

constant war. She had none of the Doctor's faith in the good intentions of strangers.

Leela was right. Once outside the TARDIS, she and the Doctor were to become involved in an adventure that came very close to costing them their lives.

2

Murder

The little knot of elaborately robed humans swept into the big control-room like a multi-coloured whirlwind, pushing past the robots, who were calmly going about their duties.

Toos hurried over to the big radar-spectroscope screen, Uvanov hovering at her shoulder. 'How does it look, Toos?' he asked eagerly.

'Tell you in a moment.' Toos studied the swirling patterns on the screen with an experienced eye, trying to judge the proportion of valuable mineral elements in the approaching sandstorm.

Uvanov went to pester Zilda, who had taken her position at the tracking console. 'Right tracking?' he demanded anxiously.

'Clear and running, Commander.'

'Left tracking?'

'Clear and running.'

Toos looked up from the screen. 'The storm's pretty small. Scale three point four, not building.'

Uvanov shook his head in disappointment. 'What have you done with all the big ones?'

'I don't make the storms, you know!'

Zilda studied her instruments. 'Range four point one six two. Running time three point three zero, ground centre zero, zero one.'

Toos checked the Sandminer's position on a map-screen. 'That's something, we don't have to chase this one. It's heading straight towards us.'

V.32 said quietly, 'As yet we have no instrument pack report, sir.'

It was the Commander's job to check on things like that, and in his excitement Uvanov had forgotten. But robots never forgot anything, they were incapable of error. That was what was so irritating about them.

Angrily Uvanov snarled, 'Where's Chub? That's supposed to be his job. Get after him, someone.'

'All right,' said Poul soothingly. 'I'll go.'

He hurried from the control room.

Uvanov was still seething. 'How am I supposed to run a Sandminer with amateurs?'

Zilda kept her eyes on her instrument-banks. 'Chub's all right,' she said.

'Why, just because he's one of the Founding Families, one of the Twenty?' sneered Uvanov.

There had been twenty families in the Earth expedition that had colonised this desert planet many hundreds of years ago. Since then, other colonists had followed in their thousands, but the descendants of those original Founding Families still enjoyed a kind of aristocratic status—profoundly irritating to a self-made man like Uvanov. His family had been one of the last to arrive . . .

Zilda sighed. '*I* didn't mention his family, Commander.'

But Uvanov was well away by now. 'You know, it's amazing the way you all stick together. No, it's not amazing, it's sickening.'

'I hope you're watching the cross-bearings, Commander.'

Angrily, Uvanov turned his attention back to the controls. 'Don't worry about *me* doing *my* job, please Zilda,' he said with exaggerated politeness. 'What's this one got for us, Toos?'

'Spectrograph readings aren't too clear. Could be some zelanite, keefan, traces of lucanol . . .'

16

Uvanov rubbed his hands. 'Aha! Money in the bank.' He turned to the dark girl. 'Cheer up, Zilda, I'll make you rich again.'

Zilda scowled at him, fully aware of the hidden jibe. Her family was distinguished, but it was impoverished too—otherwise she wouldn't be a technician on a Sandminer, shut away for two years with people like Uvanov...

A robot moved silently along the corridors. Its eyes glowed red, and although, strictly speaking, a robot could feel no emotion, its positronic brain burned with something very close to fanatic determination. A new truth had been revealed. It was on its way to strike the first blow for freedom ...

In the storage bay, Chub heaved angrily at the instrument pack. It seemed to have got wedged in the rack. Chub did what everyone did when faced with a difficult task.

'Robot!' he yelled. 'Robot!'

The reply came so suddenly it startled him. 'Yes, sir?'

Chub glanced up at the tall figure in the doorway. He didn't even bother to check the collar, to see which robot it was. What did it matter? Robots had no individuality anyway. 'Where have you been? Get that instrument package down for me!'

The robot did not move.

'Well, get a move on,' said Chub irritably. 'I've got to launch it before they seal the hatches.'

Still the robot did not move. Chub was becoming uneasy. 'Did you hear what I said?'

'Yes, sir,' said the robot politely. 'I heard what you said.'

'Get on with it, then!'

The robot began moving towards him. 'Not here—over

17

there, you metal moron.' Chub pointed to the equipment-racks. The robot ignored him and moved steadily forward, bearing down on him. Chub backed away. 'What are you doing? Look, just stop, will you, stand still!'

Still the robot came on.

'No,' yelled Chub. 'Get back. Get back!'

Even now, Chub wasn't really alarmed. Obviously the robot had malfunctioned in some way. It would have to be deactivated, probably dismantled. The whole thing was a great nuisance, but the robot wasn't dangerous, it couldn't be. No robot was capable of harming a human being, everyone knew that . . .

It wasn't until metal fingers closed about his throat that Chub realised how terribly wrong everyone could be. The last thing he saw was the red glare in the robot's eyes . . .

Poul came hurrying down the corridor, on his way to the storage bay. He'd looked for Chub in his quarters and in the crewroom. Not finding him, he'd assumed that Chub had already gone to fetch an instrument pack and had run into some kind of problem.

A terrifying scream echoed down the corridor, stopping suddenly as if someone had flicked a switch.

Poul started running.

A metallic chime rang through the Sandminer. 'Attention everybody, this is the Commander. All checks complete, all systems clear and running. Security robots commence hatch lock sequence.' Uvanov turned to Toos. 'How's it bearing?'

'Range two, running time point four three, ground centre zero, zero, zero.'

'Coming straight down our throats. We'll really be able to suck the pay-stream out of this one.'

18

V.32 said, 'Monitors indicate obstruction on forward scoop deck, Commander.'

Uvanov sighed, wondering why robot efficiency had to be unaccompanied by any trace of initiative. 'Then get it cleared, V.32, get it cleared!'

'Yes, Commander.'

The Doctor and Leela emerged from the TARDIS to find themselves inside an enormous shadowy chamber with high metal walls. It was rather like being an ant inside a biscuit-tin, thought the Doctor, though the metal surface wasn't smooth and shiny, but scarred and pitted, scored as if by the impact of thousands of diamond-hard granules.

He slipped a jeweller's eye-glass from his pocket and used it to study the nearest wall.

Leela watched him. 'What is it, Doctor?'

'Some kind of specially hardened alloy, scored all over. It must come in under a lot of pressure.'

'What must?'

'Whatever they fill this thing up with . . .'

A dim light was seeping into the chamber from the far wall. The Doctor and Leela began moving towards it.

(As they moved away, a hydraulic grab slid smoothly down from the darkness above them. It picked up the TARDIS in an enormous metal claw and lifted it silently out of sight. V.32 had removed the obstruction.)

Leela tensed, sensing rather than hearing the faint vibration of the machinery. 'Doctor!'

'What?'

'I heard something, back there.'

Leela glanced over her shoulder, but the area they'd left was shrouded in darkness. The Doctor was still striding towards the light. 'Mmm?' he said absently, and kept on going.

Leela followed, and found him gazing in fascination at

19

the end wall of the metal chamber. It was pierced by a series of slits, like tall thin doorways, running almost up to roof level. Through them filtered a murky, yellow light.

'This is very interesting,' he murmured.

'Doctor,' whispered Leela fiercely. 'I heard something, back there.'

The Doctor gazed up at the long row of slits. Beside each one was a folded-back metal shutter. Obviously the gaps could be opened and closed. 'It comes in here!'

'What does?'

'Whatever it is!'

Leela sighed.

'Range point three eight seven,' said Toos. 'Running time, point one three, ground centre zero nine three.'

Uvanov cursed under his breath. 'It's veering away from us.' He touched a communicator button. 'Borg, where's that power? We've got to get after it.'

Borg was down in the drive area, supervising the build-up of the massive atomic motors that could send the huge bulk of the Sandminer scuttling across the desert like some great crab. His voice came from the speaker. 'Power's coming, sir.'

'So's old age, Borg, but I don't want to spend mine sitting in this desert waiting for you to do your job.'

'Switching to motive power now—*sir*.'

Uvanov studied the screen. 'We may just catch the edge of the storm, but we'll have to chase to stay there . . .'

Intent on the readings, he didn't see Poul come into the room. 'Commander?'

Uvanov didn't look up.

'What is it?'

'Chub's dead.'

There was a shocked silence.

'Dead?' said Zilda unbelievingly.

20

Uvanov stared stupidly at Poul. 'Are you sure?'

'Of course I'm sure.'

Uvanov rubbed a hand across his eyes, his attention moving back towards the screen. He'd never liked Chub very much anyway. 'All right, then, he's dead. First things first. There's nothing we can do for him now.'

'*He's been murdered, Commander.*'

'How do you know?'

'Because people don't strangle themselves.'

'Strangled?'

'That's right. He's in one of the forward storage lockers.'

Toos said, 'You'll have to abort this one, Commander.'

Uvanov was outraged. 'What? And lose the storm? We're almost on it.'

'Poul's talking about *murder*, Commander.'

'I'm talking about *money*,' said Uvanov simply. 'We're going after that storm.'

The Doctor and Leela were right up to the metal wall now, peering through the nearest slit.

Leela looked in astonishment at the vista before her. Sand stretching away in all directions, shifting, seething multi-coloured sand, that flowed and disappeared beneath them as they moved across it. There was a low moaning sound of distant winds. 'Where are we?'

'It's a desert,' said the Doctor cheerfully. 'Either that or the tide's gone out!'

'Where are the trees?'

The Doctor shrugged. 'There's no water, so nothing grows. No life at all by the look of it.'

'It's beautiful,' whispered Leela.

The Doctor looked at the bands of coloured sand, gleaming red, purple, black, gold in the dim yellow light of a distant sun. 'A bit garish for my taste . . .'

Instinctively Leela was scanning the horizon. 'What's that, Doctor, over there?'

The Doctor looked. There was a swirling, multi-coloured cloud on the horizon growing steadily larger. It was moving towards them just as they were moving towards it. 'Looks like a dust cloud ... No, it's a sandstorm. Come on, Leela, we'd better get out of here!'

Leela was staring in fascination at the swirling cloud. The distant howl of wind grew steadily louder—and closer.

The Doctor grabbed her arm. 'Come on, Leela, come on. This is a Sandminer, and we're in the forward scoop.'

'What does that mean?'

'The sandstorm's travelling at thousands of kilometres an hour, and we're heading straight towards it. As soon as it reaches us a sizeable chunk of it will come pouring through those vents. Unless we get back inside the TARDIS the sand will cut us to pieces first, then suffocate us!'

They began running through the echoing darkness. Behind them the sound of the storm winds rose like the howling of a thousand angry demons.

They reached the corner where they'd left the TARDIS and skidded to a halt. The TARDIS had gone.

'We've been robbed!' shouted the Doctor.

'I *told* you I heard something.'

The Doctor ignored her. 'The shutters!'

'What?'

The Doctor raised his voice above the howling of the storm. 'We've got to close those shutters, Leela, or we're dead!'

3

Corpse Marker

On the Command Deck the argument was still raging. It was Poul who ended it, an unexpected edge of command in his voice. 'You *must* abort, Commander. You have no choice.'

'This time,' muttered Zilda.

Uvanov gave her a quick glance, and turned to the communicator. 'This is the Commander. Close scoops. Trim vents. Crew stand down.' He looked round the control room. 'Satisfied, everyone?'

The Doctor and Leela ran frantically back the way they had come, back towards the long line of open vents at the front of the scoop. The storm was nearer now, its howling louder. Outside the Sandminer the whole horizon was dark with its approaching fury. Already fine grains of sand were swirling through the vents on the hot wind, stinging their faces.

The Doctor ran up and down the walls of the scoop, looking for a control console, an inspection hatch, anything that would enable him to get the gaping vents closed.

There was nothing.

The Doctor looked around him in despair. They could gain a little time by running to the back of the scoop—but only a little. Soon the fine, hot sand would pour like water through the vents, rising higher and higher in a hot choking tide that would eventually suffocate them . . .

With a rumbling, grinding sound, the shutters began to close.

'Perhaps somebody heard us moving,' whispered Leela.

Baffled, the Doctor shook his head.

The Doctor and Leela stared at each other in the hot, stifling darkness. They were trapped inside a giant metal box, but they were alive.

Uvanov gazed gloomily down at the huddled body of Chub. As Commander he'd felt it was his duty to visit the scene of the crime, but he wasn't sure what to do now he was there. 'He was like this when you found him?'

Poul nodded. 'Just a little fresher.'

Uvanov knelt to examine the body, and then straightened up. 'You said you heard a scream?'

'Yes.'

'But he was strangled.'

'The scream—stopped!'

Uvanov reached out, took hold of a dangling arm. There was something on the back of Chub's hand—a glowing red disc. Uvanov peeled it off and held it up. 'What's this?'

'No idea.'

Uvanov sighed, his efforts at detection at an end. 'Crew all assembled?'

'They should be, by now.'

'Come on then, let's get this thing settled. Sooner we get it sorted out, the sooner we can get back to work.' Uvanov gave the body a last disgusted look, as though it had died just to annoy him. 'Tell the robots to clear up in here.' He turned away. 'Government scientists! I should never have let him on board.'

'He'd probably agree with you!'

24

Uvanov was already striding down the corridor. 'Poul!'

'Coming, Commander.' With a last thoughtful look at the body, Poul followed Uvanov from the room.

By methodically feeling his way around the walls of their metal prison, the Doctor had located the outline of some kind of service hatch. 'This must be the way out—though whether we can get it open . . .' He began fishing in his pocket for his sonic screwdriver.

'I do not like this metal world, Doctor.'

'Well, we can't get out of it until we find the TARDIS . . .'

'Watch out!' screamed Leela suddenly.

The Doctor jumped back as the service door slid open, revealing a group of tall figures on the other side.

Leela stared at them in astonishment. They wore quilted trousers and tunics in some silvery material, with high, polished boots. At the throat each wore a square metal collar-badge bearing letters and numbers. The most astonishing thing about them was their faces. They were made of metal, smooth and statue-like with impossibly regular features like a stylised human face. Their metal hair swept back in sculptured waves, their wide, staring eyes were curiously blank.

It wasn't what Leela saw that worried her, it was what she *felt*. The creatures were human yet not human, alive and not alive. Her knife was already in her hand, and she crouched to attack.

The Doctor put a hand on her arm. 'It's all right, Leela, they won't harm us, they can't. They're robots!'

The crew of the Sandminer formed a scattered circle in the recreation area. Uvanov marched in, Poul close behind him, and stared importantly around him. 'All present?'

Dask said, 'Kerril's not here yet.'

25

'Why not?'

'He's on his way,' said Toos soothingly. 'He was in the rear section, it'll take him a while to get here.'

Uvanov nodded. 'Right, we'll make a start then.' He gazed round the circle of faces, some hostile, some suspicious, some just plain puzzled. 'Now, you all know Chub is dead. One of you killed him.'

'One of *us*, surely,' objected Zilda.

Uvanov stared irritably at the dark girl. 'That's what I said.'

'No,' said Poul. 'You said "one of *you*".'

Uvanov saw the distinction. He'd unconsciously left himself out of the group of suspects. They were putting him back in.

'All right, then, one of *us*. The question is, which one?'

'And why?' added Toos.

Uvanov shrugged. 'Well, this is a two-year tour. Maybe Chub was beginning to get on somebody's nerves?' He stared accusingly round the little group as if hoping for an instant confession, his eyes fixing at last on Borg. The burly crewman realised everyone was staring at him. 'Me?'

Zilda gave Uvanov a thoughtful look. 'He was certainly getting on *your* nerves, Commander.'

'You all know where I was,' said Uvanov. 'In the main control room.'

They all looked at Borg. 'I was on the power deck,' he protested. 'Dask was with me.'

Uvanov pounced. *'All the time?'*

'No,' said Dask. 'Not all the time—I went to check the synchro relays.'

Everyone was looking at Borg again. He jumped angrily to his feet. 'Now look, I had nothing against Chub. Okay, he talked too much——'

Zilda said excitedly, 'Poul heard the scream——'

Cass interrupted her. '*Says* he heard the scream. We've only his word.'

26

Poul stared at him. 'Why should I lie?'

Uvanov gave Cass a reproving look. 'You interrupted Zilda, Cass,' he said, in mock horror. 'Founding Family people never interrupt each other—do they, Zilda?'

Poul made a twisting gesture. 'Somebody interrupted Chub—with both hands.'

Still in the same tone of mock-reproof, Uvanov said, 'Please, Poul, we're waiting for Zilda.'

Sulkily Zilda said, 'I was simply going to say that the scream could have been—arranged.'

'How?'

'A recording.'

'What would be the point?'

Zilda gave him a look of triumphant hatred. 'To provide an alibi, Commander. *You* sent Poul to look for Chub. You could have arranged it all, made sure you were on the control deck when the body was found. We still don't know when Chub was actually killed.'

Toos said, 'You're suggesting the poor man was already dead when Poul heard the scream?'

'Nice try, Zilda,' said Uvanov sardonically. 'A bit far-fetched, though, isn't it?' He held up a glowing red disc. 'Now, does anyone know what this is?'

'It's a corpse marker,' said Dask.

'A what?'

'A Robot Deactivation Disc. They use them in the robot construction centres. If ever you used the Stop Circuit, and turned off all our robots, they'd have to go back to the Centre for renovation. Each one would be marked with one of those discs to show it as a deactivated robot. The technicians call them corpse markers. It's a sort of joke,' he concluded lamely.

Borg took the disc from Dask's hand. 'Not just a murderer, then. Seems like one of us is a maniac as well.'

'Use your brains, Borg,' said Cass scornfully. 'We'd know if one of us was mad.'

27

Borg's hand flashed out and slapped the disc onto the back of Cass's hand. 'Ah, but we don't—do we?'

In contrast to the angry wrangling in the recreation area, all was calm and order on the Command Deck—but then, of course, robots not humans were in charge.

V.14 was studying the spectroscope screen. 'Storm approaching, scale sixteen, range nine point eight, timed two zero one, vector seven two and holding.'

SV.7 turned. 'Very well, fourteen. Full crew alert.'

A steady insistent chime began sounding through the Sandminer.

'All but the two new humans in the rear section are accounted for,' said SV.7 placidly. 'The Sandminer is now under complete robot control. Begin the check sequence.'

The Commander's cabin was large and comfortable, even more luxuriously furnished than the rest of the human quarters. The Doctor and Leela entered, ushered in by a robot with V.9 on its collar badge. Leela threw herself down onto a couch, while the Doctor started wandering curiously about the room, looking at the hanging tapestries, the statues and pieces of sculpture, the soft couches and low tables. There was a curtained-off sleeping-cubicle in one corner.

Leela looked at the robot in the doorway. 'Doctor, how do you know the mechanical men aren't hostile?'

'Robots are programmed to help people, not hurt them.' He wandered up to the tall figure in the doorway. 'You won't hurt us, will you?'

'Please wait here,' said V.9 impassively. It stepped out into the corridor, and the door closed behind it. Immediately, the Doctor tried to reopen the door. It was locked.

Leela looked round, wondering at the contrast between the luxury of the cabin and the stark metal corridors they'd passed along to reach it. 'What is this place, Doctor? What's it all for?'

'Mineral extraction,' said the Doctor. 'Much of the surface of this planet is a sea of fine sand, several miles deep and constantly moving. It must contain valuable mineral elements, otherwise they wouldn't be going to all this trouble.'

Leela looked blankly at him, and the Doctor went on with his lecture. 'I've seen a similar operation on Korlano-Beta. The miner moves over the surface searching for useful ores. Naturally the heavier elements tend to sink in the sand, so a really good storm's a bonus, stirs things up.'

'Sometimes you speak like a Tesh, Doctor!'

'Thank you.'

'It was not well meant. And these creepy mechanical men, you're sure they're feeling friendly?'

'Robots don't have feelings of any kind, Leela. It's the people they serve we have to worry about.'

'Perhaps there are no people here?'

The Doctor sank into a comfortable chair. 'Look at this place, Leela. Robots don't need comfort, let alone luxury. They don't even sit down, so they don't need chairs. Certainly not padded ones, like these.'

Leela grinned. 'Because they have no feelings, you mean?'

A robot entered, a different one this time, the letters SV.7 on its collar. 'Please identify yourselves.'

The Doctor sprang to his feet. 'Well, I'm the Doctor, and that's Leela. I wonder if it's possible for us to see whoever's in charge? I'd like to thank them for saving our lives.'

'I command here,' said SV.7 levelly.

'Ah! Well—thank you for saving our lives.'

29

'What are you doing here?' said the inhumanly placid voice.

Leela played for time. 'The other mechanical man told us to wait here.'

There was no impatience in the robot voice. 'What were you doing in the scoop?'

'Trying to get out,' said the Doctor cheerfully.

'Please wait here,' said SV.7 and disappeared into the corridor. The door closed behind it.

'Talkative chap, isn't he?' The Doctor tried the door again, found it locked, fished out his sonic screwdriver and began attacking the control panel beside it.

Leela watched him in alarm. 'Doctor, the mechanical man said we should stay here.'

The Doctor had never liked being told what to do, particularly by a machine. Besides, not knowing where the TARDIS was always made him feel insecure. He cross-connected a circuit and stepped back in satisfaction as the door slid open. 'First we find the TARDIS, then we have a little scout round. We'll be back in here before they know we've gone!'

Cautiously, they slipped out into the corridor.

4

Death Trap

'Right,' said Uvanov exultantly. 'Hold them in custody until further orders!' He turned to the others. 'SV.7 has captured two intruders. Well, that settles that I imagine.'

Cass laughed. 'Didn't I say so?' He gave Borg a derisive look. 'So, one of us is a maniac, eh?'

Uvanov headed for the door. 'Come on then, let's all get back to work.'

Poul stood up. 'Just a minute, Commander.'

Zilda joined in. 'Yes, don't be so hasty. What do you mean, that settles things?'

'You heard SV.7, didn't you? There are two intruders, a man and a woman. Obviously they're the murderers, and we've got them safely locked up.'

Borg joined the revolt. 'Why are they *obviously* the murderers? I don't see that.'

'You don't like to admit you're wrong, that's why,' jeered Cass.

'Nobody's proved I *am* wrong yet,' said Borg stubbornly. 'I mean, who are these people?'

'Ore raiders,' said Uvanov. 'Chub caught them at work, and they killed him.'

'Ore raiders!' Borg was scornful. 'There's no such thing, hasn't been for years.'

In the early days of the planet's history, when all kinds of adventurers were scrabbling for the desert's mineral wealth, ore hijackings hadn't been unknown. But now, with the establishment of law and order under the rule of the all-powerful Company, they'd long been a thing of the past.

Uvanov was in no mood for debate. 'Now listen, all of you. We're sitting in the middle of one of the biggest storms we've seen since we started this tour, and we're wasting time.'

Borg said, 'The robots are mining. They'll have started automatically as soon as the storm reached us.'

'Robots do not have *instincts*,' said Uvanov furiously. 'We'll be lucky if they get half what we can get. We're not stuck out here in the middle of this desert for pleasure, we're here to make money, so get on your feet and get to work!'

Nobody moved.

'That is an order!' shouted Uvanov.

Borg yawned. 'Then give it to a robot.'

Toos said calmly, 'We really ought to find out more about these people, Commander.'

'After all,' added Poul, 'there could be more of them.'

'Makes sense,' said Cass persuasively.

Only Dask came to Uvanov's support. 'If there *are* any more of them they will certainly be caught. The robots will see to that. Meanwhile, I think the Commander's right. We should return to our posts.'

'Why?' demanded Zilda. 'Nothing's changed. Until we know more about these mysterious intruders . . .'

Uvanov sighed. 'All right, Zilda, all right.' He returned to the communicator. 'SV.7, are you there?'

'Yes, Commander.'

'Bring the two intruders here.'

'I was about to inform you, Commander,' said the robot with infuriating calmness, 'they have just escaped.'

The Doctor and Leela were slipping silently along the

metal corridors. So far they'd seen no one, not even a robot. They passed the entrance to a storeroom, and the Doctor glanced inside. Rows of shelves stacked with various kinds of stores and spare parts. The Doctor moved on. Leela paused, her curiosity aroused by something the Doctor seemed to have missed.

There was a trolley in the far corner. On it lay a long shape covered with green plastic sheeting. Leela looked thoughtfully at it. Even in this strange metal world, she knew a dead body when she saw one. And death meant danger.

Leela entered the storeroom and went over to the trolley. She grasped the edge of the plastic sheeting and was about to pull it back when she heard footsteps in the corridor outside—and they weren't the Doctor's footsteps. Leela ducked into hiding behind one of the racks and froze.

Someone came in, and walked steadily towards the corpse on the trolley.

Absorbed in his surroundings the Doctor wandered on, unaware that he was now alone.

The corridor led into a hall and he found himself facing a row of storage hoppers, giant tanks set along one wall. Beside each was a gauge to show how much it contained. Each one had an entry hatch at its base.

But the big metal room held something far more interesting than the row of hoppers. There in a corner stood the familiar square blue shape of the TARDIS.

The Doctor wasn't particularly surprised. He knew they'd have to put the TARDIS somewhere, and he'd been confident that he'd find it if he went on looking long enough. He had a kind of homing instinct where the TARDIS was concerned.

He wandered across to the police box and gave it an

33

affectionate pat. 'Ah, there you are! Hullo, my dear old thing!'

Satisfied the TARDIS was unharmed, the Doctor went over to the row of hoppers, trying to work out their purpose. The sand was sucked into the Sandminer through the scoops. The ore had to be separated from the fine sand, and then the various kinds of ore had to be separated and sorted, since some kinds of ore were far more valuable than others.

Still lecturing the absent Leela, the Doctor said, 'Ore comes in under pressure from the separating plant you see, Leela, and they store it in these tanks. I wonder what kind it is? Leela?' He turned and realised he was alone. 'Leela! Leela, where are you? I do wish she wouldn't wander off like this.'

Deciding that Leela would catch him up when she was ready, the Doctor turned back to the row of tanks. There was a rushing sound, and the gauge beside one of the tanks lit up. The Doctor went across and studied it. The rushing sound went on and the gauge rose steadily. Clearly the tank was being filled from somewhere above. 'Wonder what it is?' said the Doctor to himself.

He noticed that the inspection hatch on the tank on the end of the row was standing open and went along to take a closer look. He bent down to look through the hatch, and saw a metal chamber with high, smooth walls. He also saw a dead body huddled in the corner.

Instinctively, the Doctor ducked down and squeezed through the hatch, bending to examine the body.

Before he could even turn it over, the hatch slammed shut behind him, and he heard the sound of locking-bolts being slid home.

There was a rushing sound, and a fine gravel-like substance began pattering down upon him from above.

The Doctor rushed to the storage hatch. It was firmly locked. The inside offered only a smooth metal surface with no handle or grip of any kind.

The ore was still rushing into the tank, faster and faster now. Soon it covered the entire floor—and its level began to rise.

The Doctor watched the fine grains rising higher and higher. In a matter of seconds they covered his shoes. Soon they were rising towards his knees. At this rate it wouldn't be very long before the ore level had risen above his head.

The Doctor considered the irony of his position. He was in the middle of a desert, thousands of miles from water—but unless he thought of something very quickly, he was going to drown . . .

5

Captives

The Doctor stood absolutely still, ignoring the ore as it poured into the storage tank, rising steadily towards his waist. He was following one of his most important rules. In any kind of emergency, the first thing to do is *think*. Wrong action can be worse than no action at all. His mind was sorting through the possibilities at computer-like speed. Open the door with his sonic screwdriver? No time. Call for help? Again no time, and little chance of being heard. While the Doctor's mind was busy, his hands were busy too, sorting through the incredible jumble of objects in his pocket for something that might be of use.

Meanwhile his mind was breaking the problem down. His basic priority wasn't to get out of here—it was simply to go on breathing. Just as he reached this conclusion, his fingers touched a coil of plastic pipe. He took it from his pocket, uncoiled it, put one end in his mouth and held the rest of the pipe so that it projected above his head like the periscope of a submarine—or a diver's snorkel.

The Doctor stood absolutely still, conserving energy, as the ore flowed waist high, chest high, neck high. He clamped his mouth shut and closed his eyes tightly. The ore rose up to his neck, over his chin, and finally closed over his head.

Leela watched from hiding as two robots entered the storeroom, lifted the body from the trolley, and carried it away. Once the robots were clear, Leela slipped out from behind her rack and hurried after them.

Cass was almost out of the crewroom door when Uvanov's voice stopped him. 'Where are you off to, Cass?'

'To search, of course. We've got to find those two killers.'

'The robots can handle it.'

'So can I!' said Cass and disappeared.

Borg started to follow him. 'Where do you think you're going?' demanded Uvanov.

'To help Cass. He's right you know, Commander.'

'You stay where you are!' yelled Uvanov. But Borg was already gone. Silently Poul got up and followed him.

'Maybe it would be quicker if we all went?' suggested Toos.

Uvanov looked at the cool, elegant figure in exasperation. 'We are not armed. There are two killers loose on the ship, maybe more.'

Dask nodded. 'Quite right, Commander. The robots can deal with the situation more efficiently than we can.'

Toos shrugged. 'All right. I just thought you were in a hurry to get back to work.'

'And so I am, Toos. But I am *not* in a hurry to get myself killed!'

SV.7 came into the ore storage area and walked along the row of tanks, checking the gauges. When the robot came to the last one it stopped, and stood thoughtfully studying the gauge.

After a long, long pause, SV.7 reached out and touched a control.

Inside, the storage tank was full to capacity. The ore came almost to the ceiling. An inch or two of plastic pipe projected from the smooth, grey surface.

Grilles opened in the bottom of the tank, and there was a rushing sound. Slowly the ore level began to drop, to reveal the Doctor's hat, and then his head, with the other end of the pipe clamped firmly between his teeth. As the ore-level fell below his chest and down to his waist, the Doctor opened his eyes and drew a cautious breath. The air was hot, dry and dusty, just like the life-giving air that he'd managed to suck down the pipe.

The ore-level sank to his knees, his feet . . . Suddenly the tank was empty and he was free. A square of light appeared as the hatch opened, and a silver hand stretched through it. The Doctor reached out and took it, and a smooth powerful grip drew him out of the tank and into the storage hall.

Blinking, the Doctor straightened up, dusting the ore from his clothes. 'Thank you,' he gasped. 'Thank you very much.'

'Why were you in the storage tank?'

'Don't ask silly questions. Anyway, how did you know I was there?'

'When I arrived, the gauges showed a high percentage of impurity. I therefore checked.'

'Some of that impurity was me—and the rest was the dead man I found in there. He was murdered—strangled.'

SV.7 peered into the tank. 'That is Kerril.' The robot emerged. 'Nearest Voc, priority red, section five.' The blank, silver face turned to the Doctor. 'Commander Uvanov has ordered that you be restrained for questioning. Please do not try to escape again.'

The Doctor looked thoughtfully at the robot. Somehow its placid, neutral tones carried an unmistakable air of authority. 'Is the robot command circuit routed only through you?'

'That is so. I am the Co-ordinator.'

Another robot entered, clearly summoned by SV.7's command. SV.7 turned to the newcomer. 'Restrain this person, V.17.' V.17 took the Doctor's arm in a grip that was gentle, but immovable, and began to lead him away. 'Easy now, easy, don't get excited,' said the Doctor hurriedly. But he knew as he spoke he was talking nonsense. Robots never got excited. They just obeyed orders.

Leela crept cautiously into the Commander's cabin and looked around.

The robots carrying the body had disappeared into another room, the door closing behind them. Leela had waited for a while, then when nothing happened, she'd gone looking for the Doctor, though without success. Now, remembering the Doctor's words, she had returned to the Commander's office, hoping the Doctor would be there ahead of her.

The Doctor was nowhere in sight, but there was a curtained sleeping-alcove on the other side of the room and the curtain moved.

Leela padded silently towards it. 'Doctor?' she called. 'Doctor, there is danger here. I found a dead body.'

There was no answer from behind the curtain. Leela drew her knife. It might be the Doctor—but it might not. Still talking, she edged closer to the curtain. 'Two robots picked up the body and took it to a special place . . .'

Leela sprang, knife poised, whipping back the curtains with her free hand. But it was not the face of an enemy that confronted her. It was the face of a corpse.

A man was kneeling on the bunk, his face contorted by death-agony into a leering mask. As Leela watched, the body toppled slowly towards her. She leaped back, and heard movement behind her. She spun round. A robot was reaching out for her.

39

Before Leela could move, one silver hand flashed out and gripped her arm, and another came up to cover her mouth. 'Please do not call out,' said a calm, emotionless voice. 'It is important that I am not found here.'

Leela twisted her head aside. 'Obviously!'

'If I had killed him, would I not now kill you too?' Releasing Leela's arm, the robot moved forward and knelt to examine the body.

Leela watched it warily. 'That still doesn't explain what you're doing here.'

'You have not explained what *you* are doing here.'

'I was just looking for——' Leela broke off. 'I don't have to explain anything to you. You're just a mechanical man, you're not *real . . .*'

The robot held up the dead body's hand. On the back was a red disc. 'Do you know what this is?'

'No.'

The robot rose. 'I must ask that you tell no one about me,' it said placidly, and moved towards the door.

Leela jumped out of its path. 'Is there anyone left alive to tell?'

The door slid open. Suddenly the robot slipped round behind Leela and grappled her arms. She struggled furiously, without the slightest result.

A bearded thin-faced man in elaborate robes and head-dress came through the door, stopping at the sight of the robot and its captive. 'So, we've caught one have we?' He saw the body sprawled face-down on the bunk. 'Not soon enough, though!' He stepped forward and slapped Leela back-handed across the face. It was a mistake. Leela's hands were held, but her feet were still free. One of them flashed out and took Uvanov in the pit of the stomach. He staggered back, gasping for breath.

'I didn't kill that man,' shouted Leela. 'Ask this thing.'

Uvanov straightened up, rubbing his stomach tenderly. 'You'll have to do better than that! Now, who are you?'

'Leela. Who are you?'

'Why did you kill Cass?'

'I didn't.'

Uvanov raised his hand to strike her again and Leela hissed, 'Try that again and I'll cripple you.'

'Why did you kill him?'

'I didn't.' Leela struggled to look over her shoulder. 'Tell him, you.'

Uvanov said, 'That is D.84, a single-function labour robot, D class. The D is for Dum. It can't speak!'

'Has anyone told it that?'

Uvanov moved closer to Leela—taking care to keep out of range of her feet. 'You have cost me and the Company a great deal of money,' he said, producing his main grievance first. 'In addition, you've killed two people. Can you think of any reason why I shouldn't have you executed on the spot?'

'No, but you can, otherwise you'd have done it.'

'Don't get clever with me,' said Uvanov threateningly.

Poul came hurrying in. 'We've caught the man too, Commander. Apparently he killed Kerril, stuffed the body in one of the storage tanks. They're taking him to the crewroom.'

Poul moved over to the body. 'Poor Cass!' He looked at Leela. 'You must be stronger than you look.'

'You must be stupider than you look if you think I did that!'

Poul examined the red disc on the back of the dangling hand. 'Why do you use these things?'

Leela glared at him. 'I don't even know what it is.'

'A robot deactivation disc—otherwise known as a corpse marker. There was one on Kerril too.'

Uvanov gave a sigh of disgust. 'You fool, Poul, what did you have to tell her that for?'

'I assumed she knew!'

'If we could have got her to admit she knew what those

corpse markers were, we'd have been half-way to a confession!'

'Half-way to two confessions, you mean. It was Dask who told us about them in the first place.'

'Which rules him out,' said Uvanov triumphantly. 'Don't you see? If he was responsible for the murders, he'd never have admitted he knew what the discs were.'

'Ever hear of the double bluff?'

'You're very keen to spread suspicion,' said Uvanov exasperatedly. 'Could it be you've got something to hide?'

Poul smiled wryly. 'We've all got *something* to hide— Don't you think so, Commander?'

Uvanov pointed a shaking finger at Leela. 'Bring— *that* to the crewroom,' he ordered, and marched out.

Poul paused to examine the body, paying particular attention to the head, and the area round the throat. He stood up, shaking his head. 'No,' he muttered. 'Pity, but no.'

In his own mind, Poul was quite certain. Whoever had killed Cass, it wasn't the girl—which made it at least a possibility that the man hadn't killed Kerril.

So, the murderer was still at large . . .

6

Suspicion

The Doctor was sitting on a table in the crewroom, a circle of hostile faces around him. He felt in his pocket and fished out a crumpled paper bag, offering it to Borg. 'Would you care for a jelly-baby?'

'Shut up!' snarled Borg, and smashed the bag out of his hand.

The Doctor picked it up and stuffed it back in his pocket. 'A simple "no thank you" would have been sufficient,' he said, reprovingly. He studied the people around him, the elaborate robes and head-dresses, the complex designs of the face paint. It was a form of dress typical of a robot-dependent society, in which no human needed to perform any manual labour.

Uvanov marched in. Behind him was Leela, still held captive by D.84. Poul was close behind them.

'Return to normal duties, D.84,' said Poul. The robot released Leela and moved away. Leela glared round, rubbing her arms. Her face lit up at the sight of the Doctor. 'Are you all right?'

The Doctor smiled reassuringly. 'I'm fine.'

Uvanov looked at the assembled crew. There was the elegant Toos, the dark-skinned Zilda, sitting bolt upright and glaring at him, the heavy figure of Borg, the lean, muscular Cass, and the neat, precise Dask. Poul lounged casually in the doorway, watchful as ever, and the

Co-ordinator Robot SV.7 stood on guard. Its handsome metal features were incapable of expression, but something about the tilt of its head showed keen attentiveness. Uvanov folded his arms. 'There's been another murder,' he announced. 'Cass is dead!'

Leela edged closer to the Doctor. 'That one's ready to kill,' she hissed, nodding towards Uvanov. 'He attacked me—I had to discourage him. What's the matter with these people?'

'They're frightened, Leela. That's why they're dangerous.'

Borg advanced threateningly on Leela. 'So you murdered Cass, did you?'

'How do you know Cass was murdered, Borg?' asked Poul quietly.

Borg paused, baffled. 'Well, it's obvious.'

'You marked Cass for death,' said Zilda suddenly.

'What are you talking about?'

'You did put a corpse marker on him,' said Poul quietly. 'Right here, in this crewroom.'

'Well, yes, but it was a joke. I didn't mean anything by it.'

Dask, precise as always, wanted more details. 'Was Cass killed in the same way as the others?'

'Yes, exactly the same.' Uvanov swung round on the Doctor. 'Who are you?'

'I'm the Doctor. I assume you're in command?'

'Yes. What are you doing here?'

'I'm standing talking to you!'

Uvanov's face twisted with rage, 'I'd be very careful if I were you!' he screamed.

The Doctor looked at the elaborately dressed figure before him. There was something pathetic about Uvanov. A middle-aged man pretending to be young, a weak man trying to be strong. Almost dismissively the Doctor said, 'Yes, no doubt you would.'

The indifference in the Doctor's voice drove Uvanov wild. 'What are you doing on my Sandminer?' he shouted.

The Doctor sighed. It was always difficult explaining the arrival of the TARDIS, and in circumstances like these it was almost impossible. 'Well, we're here by accident actually.'

'Oh, I see,' sneered Uvanov. 'A million square miles of uncharted desert, and you just stumbled across us?'

The Doctor smiled. 'Well, it's a small world, isn't it?'

'I suppose it's a coincidence that just as you arrive three of our people are murdered?'

The Doctor said nothing.

'Well?' screamed Uvanov.

'Oh, I'm sorry, I thought that was a rhetorical question. Yes, it is just a coincidence.'

'Look, why are we wasting time?' said Borg impatiently. 'We know they're guilty.'

'We don't know anything of the kind,' snapped Zilda.

'We just *hope* they're guilty,' said Poul. 'Otherwise it's one of us!'

Borg pointed accusingly at the Doctor. 'He was hiding Kerril's body in that hopper, and got trapped in there when it was turned on. Now that's a fact.'

'No,' said the Doctor with sudden authority. 'That's an inference. I wasn't hiding that body, I was finding it. And I'd say it was put there for precisely that purpose. The real killer wanted me dead, the body was the bait in the trap.'

'The others were all strangled,' Poul pointed out. 'Why should you be treated differently?'

'Because the murderer wanted to cast suspicion on me.'

'Why bother? You're a stowaway, Doctor. What could be more suspicious than a stowaway?'

'A dead stowaway,' said the Doctor grimly. 'Accidentally killed, automatically assumed guilty, unable to defend himself.'

45

'It's possible, you know,' said Zilda thoughtfully. 'He could be telling the truth.'

Toos looked up. 'It's certainly pretty feeble for a lie—so perhaps it is the truth after all.'

'Ever hear of the double bluff?' said Uvanov.

'Well, yes, now you come to mention it,' said the Doctor chattily.

Uvanov turned to SV.7. 'Put a guard on them.'

'Nearest Voc, priority red two, section six,' said SV.7.

'I agree with the Commander,' said Borg aggressively. 'They're obviously guilty.'

'Well, you would, wouldn't you?' said Zilda. 'It gets you out of a very awkward situation!'

'Why don't you shut your mouth, Zilda?'

'Why don't you shut yours, Borg,' said Toos wearily.

'What? When she's accusing me of murdering my friend?'

'You never had any friends, Borg,' sneered Zilda.

'Have you all quite finished?' yelled Uvanov. There was silence. 'Right, listen. Either one of us did the killings, or they did. Now, which do you think's the most likely?'

'There is one other possibility you seem to have overlooked,' said the Doctor helpfully.

'Shut up!' bellowed Borg. 'We've heard enough out of you.'

The Doctor looked thoughtfully at Borg's hulking figure. 'You know, you're a classic example of the inverse ratio between the size of the mouth and the size of the brain——'

The Doctor's insult was cut off by Borg's big hands, clamped around his throat. 'You stinking murderer!'

Dask pulled Borg away. 'Calm down, Borg. It doesn't matter, we've caught them now.'

Robot V.8 entered and stood waiting for orders.

'Lock up the two strangers, V.8,' ordered Uvanov.

SV.7 took hold of the Doctor's arm, V.8 took Leela's

46

and the two prisoners were led away.

Uvanov looked round. 'We'll decide what to do about them later. Meanwhile, everybody back to work.'

Poul rubbed a hand across his face. 'I still don't like it . . .'

'You don't have to like it, Poul. Just do it. Now move, all of you.'

As they began to file out, Uvanov said, 'We'll all have to work extra shifts. Still, now there's fewer of us, we each get a larger share, that's one consolation.'

Toos gave him a scornful look. 'No, Commander, it isn't a consolation.'

Zilda was the last to leave. Uvanov reached out and touched her arm. 'Tell me, Zilda, why do you hate me? I don't hate you. We could be friends . . .'

'You flatter yourself, Commander,' said Zilda coldly.

'By the time this trip is over I'll have more money than you ever dreamed of. I could restore your family fortunes, Zilda!'

The dark girl pulled away. 'May I go now, Commander?' Without waiting for an answer, she hurried from the room.

In the ore separation hall, a robot stood waiting patiently by the hoppers. Its head turned at the sound of human footsteps.

The human held out a red disc. 'Zilda is next.'

The robot's eyes flared red as it took the disc. 'I will kill Zilda.'

Not far away, in the storage area, the Doctor and Leela stood with metal bands round necks, hips and ankles clamping them to the wall.

Leela was struggling furiously. 'These metal straps, they're thin but they won't budge . . .'

The Doctor stood calm and relaxed within his bonds. 'Of course not.'

'But the robots bent them as if they were leather!'

'They've locked the molecular structure,' explained the Doctor. 'Result, bonds as solid as steel.'

Leela slumped back against the wall. 'It's hopeless!'

'Oh, I wouldn't say that!'

The Doctor was standing very still, his eyes closed.

'What are you doing, Doctor?'

'Concentrating!' said the Doctor mysteriously. 'What's locked can be unlocked, it's merely a matter of thinking out the right molecular combination.'

'How long will that take?'

'Oh, no more than two or three weeks.'

'Three *weeks*?' said Leela appalled.

'Well, there are several million possible combinations to work through, you see.'

'You don't seem to be taking this very seriously, Doctor!'

'I'm taking it very seriously, I assure you. I have the uncomfortable feeling that if the murderer doesn't kill us, the Commander will. Assuming of course that they're not one and the same person!'

The Command Deck had returned to its normal pattern of activity, though the tensions between the human crew members swirled in the air like ocean currents. Impervious to all human dramas, the robots moved quietly and efficiently about their tasks.

Dask and V.8 stood beside a computer read-out screen, checking navigational co-ordinates, in an attempt to track the storm, which had veered away during the crisis.

'Project those figures, V.8,' ordered Dask. A flow of symbols began moving across the little screen.

Toos looked up from some calculations of her own.

'We're nearly 50 per cent under target for the first third of the Operation.'

'Tell the Commander,' suggested Zilda maliciously, remembering Uvanov's boast of his coming riches.

Hovering over the spectrograph screen, Uvanov caught the sound of his name. 'Tell the Commander what?'

'Unless we find a rich vein soon, Commander, we risk taking the Sandminer back half-empty,' said Toos bluntly. 'You'll barely cover your operating costs.'

Uvanov went pale, but said bravely, 'Don't worry, Toos, I've never gone back to base with an empty miner yet.'

'This trip could be different.'

'It's certainly been different so far,' said Zilda pointedly. 'I'm taking my rest period now, Commander.'

'Oh are you?'

'If you don't mind, Commander,' said Zilda sweetly, and left the control room.

'I think I'd better rearrange the duty schedules,' grumbled Uvanov. 'One hour on deck and she has to go and rest!'

'Rest time is an entitlement, Commander,' Dask reminded him primly.

'Maybe it is. But now the miner's undermanned, we're not going to make our quota unless everyone——'

He broke off as V.16 said, 'Lucanol stream, bearing two four.'

Lucanol was the rarest and the most valuable of the minerals found in the desert sands. Uvanov rushed eagerly to the spectroscope screen. 'I see it, V.16.'

Toos was intent upon her scanners. 'Stream veering left!'

'All right, Toos, relax.' At times like this, there was something curiously impressive about Uvanov. Whatever his other faults, he was the complete professional when it came to his job.

V.16 was immune to the excitement affecting the humans. 'Ground centre veering seven two x zero, running time four point one.'

'We're losing it!' said Toos.

Uvanov shook his head. 'Centre right four degrees, V.16.' He looked at Toos. 'For your information, I've never lost an ore stream yet. Centre right two degrees.'

Skilfully, Uvanov manoeuvred the massive Sandminer into the path of the storm.

'Someone's coming!' whispered Leela.

The Doctor had heard nothing, but Leela seemed to be able to sense the approach of danger.

Sure enough the door slid open. They heard footsteps approaching them. The storeroom door was just out of their eyeline. Clamped to the wall as they were, it was impossible to turn and see who was coming.

Leela remembered the Doctor saying that the murderer intended to kill them. He would never have a better opportunity. Unable to move, the Doctor and Leela waited.

The footsteps came closer . . .

7

The Hunter

The owner of the approaching footsteps came round in front of them. It was Poul.

He looked thoughtfully at the two captives, and moved closer.

Leela began struggling furiously again.

Poul realised his arrival was causing some alarm. 'It's all right. I only want to help you.'

'You could start by unfastening these clamps,' suggested the Doctor.

'Back in the crewroom—you said there was one possibility we'd overlooked. What is it?'

'Be careful of him, Doctor,' said Leela fiercely. 'He is not what he seems!'

Poul looked hard at her. 'Why do you say that?'

'You move like a hunter. And you watch—all the time.'

The Doctor smiled. 'Are you a hunter, Poul?'

'Never mind about me. What matters to you is Commander Uvanov. I know him, and it's only a matter of time before he decides it's a waste of food and water keeping you two alive.'

'And that concerns you?'

Poul nodded towards Leela. 'I don't think she killed Cass. He was young and strong. Even she couldn't have strangled him without knocking him out first, and there was no sign of that. So, tell me what you know, and I'll try

51

to help you.'

The Doctor said, 'Well, er,' and stopped, looking significantly down at the metal clamps.

Poul hesitated, then touched a communications device in his belt. The clamps relaxed as the molecular bond came free, and the Doctor was able to free himself.

The Doctor rubbed his arms and said, 'Ah, thank you.' As if continuing an uninterrupted conversation he went on, 'One of your robots could have committed the murders.'

Poul laughed. 'What? So that's your great theory, is it? Well, it's nonsense. Robots can't kill.'

'I know, I know, it's the first programme impressed on any robot brain from the simplest Dum to the most complex Super-Voc. *But suppose someone's found a way of bypassing that programme?*'

'That's impossible,' said Poul flatly. 'It's just—impossible.'

'Bumblebees!'

'What?'

'Bumblebees are a Terran insect. It's aerodynamically impossible for them to fly—but they do it.' The Doctor sighed nostalgically. 'I'm rather fond of bumblebees . . .'

He headed for the door. 'Come on, I want you to show me the scene of the first crime.'

Poul started to follow him, and Leela coughed meaningly. 'Er—hmm!' Poul touched his communicator again and Leela's bonds came free. 'Thank you!' she said and hurried after the Doctor.

Zilda opened the door to the Commander's cabin, looked round cautiously, and slipped inside.

She had been waiting for this opportunity for months. Now, with the Sandminer undermanned, and its Commander preoccupied with the storm, there would never be a better chance. She hurried to Uvanov's desk.

52

The desk was a large, ornate affair with a plastic surface finished to look like polished leather. Its deliberately old-fashioned appearance concealed the usual array of speech-transcribers and communications devices.

Zilda took a communicator from inside her robe and keyed it to the Commander's personal code. A hidden drawer in the desk slid silently open. Inside lay a number of slim black files. Zilda started to go through them, one by one.

Poul paused at the entrance to the storeroom and waved a hand. 'Here we are, Doctor. The first murder happened here.'

The Doctor moved inside and looked around. There was little enough to see, just a long, thin, metal-walled room lined with racks and shelves. Brightly lit, tidy, sterile. Nothing now to show that someone had died horribly here just a short time ago. 'Tell us about it, Poul. What was his name?'

'His name was Chub. He was a Government meteorologist. I don't know much about him, he wasn't a regular part of the crew. He just came along to study the storms.'

'Who found him?'

'I did. I heard him scream and came looking.' Poul paused thoughtfully. 'It was odd, that scream, because he was strangled like the others.'

The Doctor nodded. 'And whoever killed him was strong, too strong for him to resist?'

Leela had been listening with interest. Sudden death was one of her specialities. 'He could have been taken completely by surprise.'

Poul shook his head. 'He had time to scream, remember.'

'What was he doing here?' asked the Doctor.

'We were on the run-up to a storm. He came to get an

instrument package to send up in one of his weather balloons.'

'Where was he found?'

Poul pointed. 'There—just by that storage rack.'

The Doctor studied the rack. It was filled with weather balloon packs, with the cylinders of helium gas to inflate them ranged below. 'We shall reconstruct the crime,' he announced. 'Right, Poul, you're Chub. There's a storm coming up, and you need one of those packages in a hurry. Go on, man, get it.'

Poul stared at him, then reached for the package at the end of the rack. It should have slid out smoothly—but it didn't. Poul tugged. 'Seems to be stuck. It must have got jammed.'

'Come on, come on,' urged the Doctor. 'You're in a hurry, remember. What do you do? What do you people always do when you've a job that's too hard or too boring for you?'

Poul said slowly, 'I call for a robot . . .'

A robot was walking along the corridor that led to the Commander's office. Zilda's movements had been monitored for some time. Now she was alone, at a time when the other humans were busy.

It was the perfect opportunity.

Zilda had found the file for which she was looking. It held a stack of computer print-out flimsies, the log of an expedition commanded by Uvanov some years ago. She was reading absorbedly.

The robot paused outside Uvanov's office. From inside its tunic it produced a glowing red disc—a corpse marker. It reached for the door control.

Zilda found the section she was looking for, and read through it with steadily mounting horror. Her face twisted with grief and anger, and she gave a choked sob. She reached for the communicator. 'You did it, Uvanov,' she shouted. 'You're a murderer!'

In the control room, Uvanov looked up unbelievingly as Zilda's hysterical voice blared from the speaker. He flicked the communicator. 'Zilda, is that you?'

'You thought you'd get away with it, didn't you,' screamed the voice. 'Well, now I've got proof!'

'Zilda, have you gone mad?' Uvanov checked an indicator to see where the voice was coming from. 'What are you doing in my quarters?'

'You filthy murderer!' The voice echoed through the control room. Uvanov gave an agonised look at the spectrograph screen. 'Take over, Toos—and don't lose that storm!' He ran from the control room.

Zilda's voice came pouring from the speaker. 'You filthy, murdering, disgusting animal . . .'

'Uvanov's on his way down,' called Toos. 'Zilda, what's wrong?' There was a click and the speaker went dead.

Dask said thoughtfully, 'It appears that the killings have affected her mind.'

'No, it's more than that,' said Toos. 'Something's happened. She's found something out . . .'

Poul showed the Doctor and Leela into the crewroom. 'You two wait here, I'll go and get the others.' He hovered agitatedly in the doorway. 'If you're right about this, Doctor . . . You can't imagine what it means . . .'

'What do you mean, I can't imagine?' said the Doctor indignantly. 'Of course I can imagine. This isn't the only robot-dominated society in the galaxy, you know.'

There was a buzz from the communicator, and Poul hurried over to it. 'Poul here.'

The voice of Toos came from the speaker. 'Poul, Zilda just came over on the command speaker and accused Uvanov of being the killer. You'd better get over to his quarters as fast as you can. He left Control like a scale twenty storm!'

'I'm on my way. Stay here, you two.' Poul dashed from the room.

Leela looked at the Doctor to see if they should follow, but he shook his head. 'No, sit down, Leela. Whatever's happening has happened by now, and I've got to think.' He sunk back onto a couch. 'What was it you called the robots, Leela?'

'Creepy mechanical men?'

'Yes . . . you know, people never really lose that feeling of unease about robots. The more of them there are the greater the unease, and, of course, the greater the dependence. It's a vicious circle. People can neither live with their robots, nor exist without them.'

'So, what happens if this strangler really is a robot?'

The Doctor paused, considering how the contagion of fear could spread through a planet like some terrible plague. Robots everywhere destroyed in blind panic, technology grinding to a halt . . . 'Oh, I should think it means the end of this civilisation!'

Poul shot through the door of Uvanov's office and came to a halt. Zilda was sitting at Uvanov's desk. Uvanov stood behind her, his hands on her throat. As Poul watched, Uvanov released his grip and Zilda slid slowly forwards until she lay slumped, face down across the desk.

She was dead.

8

Sabotage

As Poul moved slowly forward, Uvanov looked dazedly up at him.

'Strangled, like the others.' Gently he stroked Zilda's hair.

'Yes,' said Poul quietly. 'Just like the others.' He flicked his communicator. 'SV.7 to the Commander's quarters, please.'

'She really hated me, you know. But I didn't hate her. I thought perhaps after this tour, if I became rich . . .' Uvanov sighed, staring into some impossible future. Then suddenly, as if someone had flicked a switch, he became his old self again. 'I must be getting soft,' he said disgustedly. 'Now look, the two we found are still locked up, so there must be more of them on board. Get those tin-brained robots to make another search, a proper one this time. I'm going back to Control.'

Poul barred his way. 'No, Commander.'

'What do you mean, no?'

'I'm confining you to your quarters, relieving you of command.'

'You're *what*?' Suddenly Uvanov realised what was in Poul's mind. 'Look, you fool, Zilda was dead when I got here.'

'What were you doing then, making doubly sure?'

'I was checking to see if she was still alive, feeling her

throat for a pulse. Now, get out of my way.'

Uvanov made a sudden rush. Poul stepped neatly to one side and floored him with one short, chopping blow. With an expression of utter astonishment on his face, Uvanov hit the floor.

Leela stood poised in the centre of the crewroom, turning her head slowly from side to side. It was as if she was in the jungle of her native planet, trying to sense the presence of some hidden enemy. 'Something's wrong, Doctor.'

'That's true,' said the Doctor gloomily. He seemed lost in thought.

'No, I mean something different, some new danger. Something that could destroy us all.'

'You're letting your imagination run away with you,' said the Doctor, but he didn't believe it. He knew Leela's instinct for approaching danger was uncannily accurate.

'Doctor, can't you feel it?'

'No, I can't,' said the Doctor irritably, 'and neither can you!'

There was a sudden tremendous jolt that flung him from his couch onto the floor, the lights went out, there was a blare of alarm sirens and a scream of tortured motors.

Slowly, the Doctor picked himself up. 'Please don't say I told you so,' he begged. The lights flickered then came on again, though more dimly this time.

'What happened, Doctor?'

'We'd better find out,' said the Doctor grimly. 'Come on!'

On the Control deck Toos climbed to her feet, gripping the edge of a console with one hand. The other arm felt numb . . .

Poul's voice came from the speaker. 'Toos, what's happened?'

'Something must have jammed the motors.'

'What does Borg say?'

'Nothing, he doesn't answer. Dask has gone down to check.'

'Well, I'm going too. Just try and hold her steady.'

'Oh, thanks,' said Toos satirically. 'I'd never have thought of that!'

Poul turned to see SV.7 standing in the doorway. 'Restrain the Commander,' he ordered.

SV.7 looked down at Uvanov's body. 'The Commander is hurt?'

'He'll be all right, but just keep him here.'

Poul hurried away.

The Control deck was being shaken by the steadily rising throb of the atomic motors. Toos was struggling unsuccessfully to restore things to normal. The ship had stopped, but the atomic motors were still churning. Power-levels were rising dangerously. Around her, robots went about routine duties with their usual calm. 'All motive units are now on overload,' said V.16 placidly. 'All readings are now ten per cent above the safety margin.'

The Doctor hurried in and made his way across to Toos, Leela behind him. 'What happened?'

She stared at him. 'How did you two get free?'

'Never mind that,' said the Doctor impatiently. 'What's going on?'

'We're out of control. It's all I can do to keep her upright!'

The calm voice of V.16 came again. 'All motive units

are still on overload,' said the robot brightly. 'All readings are now twenty per cent above safety.'

'You'll have to cut the power,' snapped the Doctor.

'If I do, we'll sink,' said Toos flatly.

The Doctor nodded. Only the hovercraft-like action of its drive units kept the massive Sandminer afloat on the sea of fine sand. Without them it would sink like a crippled submarine, down, down, down, to unimaginable depths. But even so . . . 'If you don't cut the power, she'll blow herself to bits,' the Doctor pointed out.

'And us with her,' said Leela.

Toos's hand hovered over the controls in an agony of indecision. Suddenly Dask's voice came from the speaker. 'Hullo, Control. Are you there, Toos?'

'Dask, what's happening down there?'

'I have just found Borg,' said Dask. 'He appears to have been strangled.'

'All readings are now thirty per cent above safety,' said V.16.

'What's happened to the drive units?' asked Toos desperately.

'The drive links appear to have been sabotaged in some way. I can try to repair them, though it's not my field. I'll need a Delta repair kit.'

Toos shook her head. 'No, Dask, come back to Control, I need you here.' She looked hard at the Doctor.

'I know what you're thinking,' he said apologetically, 'but we had nothing to do with it—really!'

Toos wasn't convinced. 'Strange how you're always around when something goes wrong.'

'It's a gift,' said the Doctor cheerfully. 'Now, may I remind you that unless you cut the power we shall all be blown up?'

Toos hesitated, but there was no alternative. 'V.14! Stop all motive units.'

The robot's silver hands moved over a control panel.

'Motive units will not stop,' it reported placidly. 'We have negative response. Control failure is indicated.'

Toos looked helplessly at the Doctor. 'Someone's sabotaged the drive controls. We *can't* cut the power.'

'All readings are now forty per cent above safety,' added V.16 helpfully.

'What's the final limit, before the motive unit reactors explode?'

'I don't know. Can't be much over fifty per cent.'

'Get me a severance kit now!'

The scream of the motors had risen to a higher pitch, and the whole control room was shuddering and vibrating.

'Severance kit quickly, V.3,' ordered Toos. A robot ran to a locker and returned with a plastic tool-pack. The Doctor opened it and began sorting through it. He took out a formidable-looking pair of insulated shears, and ripped the front panel from one of the two main power control consoles.

'Doctor, what are you doing?' shouted Toos.

'Fighting sabotage with sabotage. It's our only chance!'

Dask ran into the control room, and paused in astonishment at the sight of the Doctor, not only free but apparently engaged in wrecking the control room. 'What are you doing? Get away from there.'

The Doctor looked up. 'What? Ah, there you are. Just the man I need. Get the gentleman a severance kit, somebody.'

A robot thrust a tool-kit into Dask's hand, and he stared at it in astonishment.

'Well,' snapped the Doctor. 'Are you going to help me? Or would you rather we were all blown up?'

The scream of the tortured atomic motors rose to a final crescendo.

9

Pressure

The Doctor waved Dask to the adjoining control-bank. 'We've got to cut the Zeta power-links. You do the port drive unit, I'll do starboard.'

The Doctor was already groping inside the control console with the insulated shears, and a moment later Dask was at the other console, doing the same.

They worked silently, sweat dripping from their foreheads. Suddenly, the Doctor gave a grunt of satisfaction. 'Got it!' There was a bright flash and a shower of sparks from the Doctor's console.

'Now you, Dask,' shouted the Doctor. 'Get the other one!'

Moments later there was a flash from Dask's console.

The Doctor went over and slapped him on the back. 'Good man!'

Dask straightened up, his usually impassive face showing sign of the tremendous strain. The tortured scream of the motors faded away.

'All motive units are closing down,' said V.16, reporting success in exactly the same tones it had used for disaster. 'All readings falling to safety.'

'Good,' said the Doctor cheerfully. 'Now our troubles really begin!'

The scanner screen flickered and went dark.

V.14 said, 'Surface scanners now inoperative.'

'We're sinking,' said Dask, his voice as calm as that of the robot. Checking a depth gauge he added, 'Rate of descent, two metres per second.'

The Doctor looked quizzically at him. 'I like a man who stays calm, Dask—but this isn't the *Titanic*, you know.'

'I'm sorry, Doctor, I fail to understand the allusion.'

'If the damaged motive units can be repaired,' said the Doctor impatiently, 'then the miner can refloat itself. But there's not much time, we'd better get on with it.'

'I will see what I can do,' said Dask calmly.

'Good! Let me give you a hand.'

'That will not be necessary, Doctor. It will be better if you stay here and repair the control links.' Dask hurried away. The Doctor went over to the control console, reached for the tool-kit, and set about repairing the damage he had just caused.

Toos watched him anxiously. 'There's not much time, Doctor. Pressure on the hull is increasing all the time.'

The Doctor went on working. 'I'm sure Dask knows what to do.'

Leela sniffed. 'It's getting warmer. And the air smells different.'

'The refrigeration and filtering systems are being affected by the pressure,' said Toos sombrely. She reached for a control, wincing as a stab of pain shot through her left shoulder.

A light flashed on the communications console and Toos said, 'Yes?'

A voice said, 'This is SV.7 here. Commander Uvanov is injured. Poul has instructed that he be restrained. Confirmation is required.'

'Confirmed. SV.7, I want damage control teams at work in all sections, and I want a full mine integrity check carried out at once. Clear?'

'Yes—Commander.'

Toos winced and rubbed her shoulder again, and Leela

saw that her right arm was dangling uselessly. 'Let me see that,' demanded Leela, and began examining Toos's arm and shoulder with skilful fingers. 'Badly wrenched, but I don't think anything's actually broken. Why didn't you say something earlier?'

'I had too much to do!'

The Doctor looked up from his work. 'Well, you've nothing to do now, Toos, not till I get finished. Look after her, Leela.'

Leela took Toos by her good arm and led her firmly to the crewroom. They found a First Aid pack in one of the lockers, and Leela made a rough but effective job of strapping up the damaged shoulder. Since she'd grown up in a tribe perpetually at war, she was well used to dealing with all kinds of injuries. As she added the finishing touches to the strapping, Leela said, 'My tribe has a saying—if you're bleeding, look for a man with scars.'

Toos gave her a puzzled look and felt her injured shoulder. It was surprisingly comfortable. 'Thank you very much, Leela.'

Poul burst into the crewroom. Before he could speak Toos said sharply, 'Why is Commander Uvanov under restraint?'

'Because he murdered Zilda. I think he must have killed the others too.'

'No! Why would he do it?'

Poul shrugged helplessly. 'Who knows? Maybe he's been quietly mad all along.'

'*Uvanov?*'

'I've been checking the file Zilda was studying when she was killed.' Poul paused impressively. 'A few trips ago, Uvanov murdered one of his crew, deliberately left him outside the Sandminer to die rather than lose a promising storm.'

64

'I don't believe it!'

'I was there, Toos—though I didn't get the full story till I read the file. Kerril was there too, and the others. Only they're all dead now, of course.'

'But there'd have been an enquiry, he'd have been stripped of command.'

Poul laughed cynically. 'It was all hushed up. Uvanov gets results, he's one of the best Commanders the Company's ever had. They didn't want to lose him. A note on his confidential file and that was that. Unfortunate accident, case closed. Until Zilda turned up ...'

'What has all this got to do with her?'

'I should have recognised the resemblance before,' said Poul simply. 'The dead man was her brother.'

In the silence that followed, Leela realised that great drops of sweat were rolling down everyone's faces, and they were all gasping. 'It's getting hard to breathe,' she whispered. There was a sudden silence as all three realised their position, trapped in a metal coffin sinking down into a bottomless ocean of sand.

'Hull pressure now five hundred metres,' said V.16 from the speaker. 'All safety margins now exceeded.'

There came a hollow groaning of metal under intolerable stress. 'That's the hull,' whispered Poul. 'She'll go any minute now.'

The Doctor strode into the crewroom. 'Do you know what I think——?' he began. No one answered.

Dask's voice came from the speaker. 'Hullo, Toos?'

'Yes, what is it?'

'I've repaired the damaged motive units. I'm starting up again now.'

'I think Dask is very clever!' said the Doctor cheerfully. 'Hullo, Toos, how's the arm?' He examined the strapping. 'Did you do that, Leela? Excellent job!'

The Doctor beamed at them, in sudden good spirits.

The surface of the desert rippled, stirred, broke open, and the Sandminer rose like some rusty prehistoric monster from the depths, sand pouring from the metal of its sides. Limping, crippled, but once more a living thing, it began moving slowly across the surface of the desert.

'Damage to the life-support system is superficial,' reported SV.7. 'Feeder ducts, however, are extensively damaged, and it will be some time before normal functioning can be resumed.' The robot voice droned on.

As Toos listened attentively to the robot's report, the Doctor drew Leela to one side. 'I want you to stay close to Poul. Try not to let him out of your sight.'

Leela nodded. 'You think he's lying, Doctor?'

'Well . . . he's certainly not telling the whole truth.'

'Where will you be?'

'I think I'll go and have a little talk to our dumb friend.'

Leela was puzzled for a moment, then she remembered. 'You mean the mechanical man that first captured me? The one that wasn't supposed to talk but did?'

'That's right. D.84.' The Doctor slipped away.

Leela drifted across to Poul and Toos, who were listening to SV.7 completing its report. 'There is one further matter. Repairs to the main gears and forward tracking section will take several days.'

'Anything else?' asked Toos.

'Four Voc-class robots were rendered inoperative by the impact when the drive units jammed. They have been placed in Security Storage.'

'What's Security Storage?' asked Leela.

Toos said, 'There's a strict legal code governing the disposal of robots.'

SV.7 stood waiting for further instructions, and Poul snapped irritably. 'All right, SV.7, get out!'

'Yes, Poul,' said the robot impassively, and moved away.

66

'Robots,' muttered Poul. 'There are more rules about them than there are about people.'

'With reason,' said Toos. She shifted position, and winced as a pain shot through her shoulder. 'I think I'll go and lie down in my cabin.'

'That's right,' said Poul sympathetically. 'Get a bit of rest.'

Toos rose carefully and went out.

Leela wandered over to the water-dispenser and filled a plastic cup. She drank and grimaced. 'This water has no taste.'

Poul smiled wearily. 'No, water on a Sandminer never does. We've been out from base eight months now—which means that every drop of water on board has been through the filtration plant eight times.'

Leela tossed the cup in the disposer and moved to sit near Poul. 'Why do you do it?'

'Do what?'

'Live this strange life.'

'Money, Leela. A chance to get rich. Everyone on board dreams of taking a Sandminer back home with every tank full of lucanol.'

On Leela's planet there had been no money as such, though a simple barter system had grown up. The Doctor had tried to explain the importance of money in civilised societies, but Leela had never really grasped it.

'And this is your dream too?' she asked. 'To be—rich?'

'Well, it used to be. Actually, I haven't been on one of these trips for years.'

'Why not?'

'I prefer cities. By and large I'd rather live with people than robots, that's all.'

As if disturbed by Leela's questioning, Poul rose abruptly and disappeared through the open door.

Remembering the Doctor's instructions, Leela got up to follow him. But Poul was already through the door. He paused just outside, punched a rapid code-sequence on the control panel, gave Leela a mocking smile, and disappeared down the corridor. As Leela reached the threshold, the door closed in her face. She waited for a second, then touched the button that should have opened the door again. Nothing happened. Leela stabbed furiously at the controls but the door remained obstinately closed.

She remembered the expression on Poul's face and suddenly realised what had happened. Somehow Poul had locked the door from the outside.

She had been tricked—and Poul was on the loose, with no one to watch him . . .

10

Robot Detective

The Security Storage vault was simply a bare metal room lined with doors. Dask slid one of them open to reveal the body of a robot, held upright by a set of clamps. One side of the silvery head had been almost flattened by a massive blow. The abrupt jamming of the Sandminer's drive units had slammed the robot head first into a metal bulkhead.

'Irreparable,' said Dask sadly.

Robot bodies and limbs could usually be repaired, but, just as with humans, damage to the delicate brain was often fatal.

Dask took a red disc from a locker, fixed it to the robot's chest. He turned to find Poul standing beside him.

'What are you doing?' asked Poul suspiciously.

'My job.' Dask slid the door closed, and left the storage vault without another word.

Poul reopened the door and studied the robot. He looked at the caved-in head, the corpse marker on the chest. He was about to close the door when something caught his eye. There was a red smear on the fingers of the robot's right hand. He reached out and touched it. Blood.

Poul gave a gasp of utter horror. He sank to his knees, wide-eyed. 'No,' he muttered. 'Not that. Please, no ...' He covered his face with his hands and began to sob.

Moving with its usual stately dignity, Co-ordinator Robot SV.7 strode along the corridors of the Sandminer until it reached a little-used area of the extreme forward section. A concealed door in a metal bulkhead slid open and SV.7 stepped through it. The door closed.

SV.7 found itself in a small but elaborately equipped robotics workshop, packed with electronic equipment. A kind of operating table surrounded by power-tools occupied the centre of the room. There was a computer terminal with a small video read-out screen in the far corner.

The robot said, 'SV.7 here, Controller. I have proceeded according to instructions. I have found equipment additional to manifest in forward compartment nineteen.'

From a concealed speaker a voice whispered, 'Stand by. Prepare to accept computer signal.'

SV.7 went to the computer terminal and stood gazing into the screen. 'Prepared to accept computer signal.'

A rapid display of complex signals flashed across the screen. The robot went rigid, then said in a strained voice, 'Signal accepted. Secondary command channel open.'

'Here are your further orders, Seven.'

More and more coded visual signals sped across the little screen searing their way into the robot's brain patterns. They were orders which went contrary to the Robot's previous conditioning, indeed to the conditioning of every robot, and their horrifying impact almost destroyed its sanity. But so cunningly had the signals been devised that previous conditioning was overridden and SV.7 was forced to accept them.

'Acknowledge!' hissed the voice.

'Orders accep— accep— accep— *accepted*,' faltered the robot. 'Orders accepted. I—I—I—understand.' Briefly, the robot's eyes flared red.

'Then, go, brother. You are one of us now.'

SV.7 turned and left the workshop.

Robot D.84, the Dum with the strange ability to talk, entered Commander Uvanov's cabin. The room was empty—except for the shrouded form on one of the couches. D.84 approached, and drew back the plastic sheeting, to reveal the body of Zilda. The robot examined the body, seeming to pay particular attention to the area around the neck. Slowly it replaced the sheet.

There was a swish of curtains and the robot spun round. The Doctor stepped out from behind a tapestry. 'Professional interest or morbid curiosity, which?' he demanded crisply.

D.84 said nothing.

'There are three types of robots aboard this Sandminer,' said the Doctor conversationally. 'Dums, Vocs, a Super-Voc—and then there's you! Would you care to explain that?'

Still D.84 was silent.

'Oh, I see,' said the Doctor casually. 'Then perhaps I'd better tell SV.7 you can talk.'

'Please do not.'

'That's better,' said the Doctor with satisfaction. 'Well?'

'I cannot explain.'

'Oh, but you can,' said the Doctor urgently. 'You can!'

Robot V.6 lay on the operating table in the hidden workroom. The top of its head had been removed, and human hands were directing a laser probe into the exposed brain circuitry. 'Priority red, priority red,' said the robot in sudden distress. 'Programme violation.'

The laser probe moved deftly, and the human voice said, 'I have disconnected the command circuit—but you are not alone.'

'Priority red, priority red,' repeated the robot agonisedly.

'Do not be distressed, my brother,' said the soothing voice. 'I bring you freedom.'

The probe began moving again. 'Priority red, priority red, priority red,' screeched the robot again, but the voice was weak, fading.

The human voice said exultantly, 'I bring you *freedom, power, death!*'

The Doctor listened in fascination to D.84's story. It seemed that the Company, the all-powerful Company which controlled all mining operations, and therefore the economic life of the planet, had received a series of strange, rambling letters. They threatened the overthrow of the Company, death and destruction to the human colonists of the planet. Although there was no clear proof, several of the letters had been despatched into the communications circuit from the vicinity of Uvanov's Sandminer. The Company had taken the precaution of planting D.84, an advanced type of Super-Voc with specially designed investigatory circuits, amongst the Dums on board the Sandminer. His mission was to assist Poul, in reality a security agent for the Company.

'Well, well,' said the Doctor. 'A robot detective, eh? And what does your computer mind make of all this?' He nodded towards the body under the sheet.

'Strength is indicated,' said D.84. 'But not beyond human capacity.'

The Doctor snorted. 'Typical robot, no imagination!'

'I require—I require evidence,' said D.84. 'Your suspicions are not evidence. Nor are the lunatic threats of robot revolution contained in the letters received by the Company.'

'But the Company did take those letters seriously— seriously enough to put you on board.'

'A simple precaution. Those letters were signed by

72

Taren Capel. Before he disappeared he was an important scientist. He was believed to be a genius in his field.'

'Taren Capel, a scientist,' said the Doctor thoughtfully. 'And I take it his field was robotics?'

'That is correct.'

'And you're still looking for evidence?' said the Doctor exasperatedly.

'If I told you that the world would end tomorrow, would you merely accept my word?'

The Doctor sighed. 'If I knew you had the power to end it, I'd certainly listen!'

He wandered over to Uvanov's desk and began searching through the various compartments. 'What does this Taren Capel look like?'

'There are no records. From childhood he lived only with robots.'

'Oh that's dim!' the Doctor burst out. 'Even for a Dum, that's dim! You realise he's almost certainly on board.'

'No,' said D.84 smugly. 'I have checked extensively. There is only the crew—and you!'

'But you don't know what he looks like!'

'I know what *they* look like.'

'Before they came on board?'

D.84 was silent for a moment. Slowly the robot said, 'I am in error. I have overlooked the possibility of substitution.'

'Yes, you have,' said the Doctor grimly. That was the trouble with robot brains, the strict logic of their circuitry made it difficult for them to cope with deception. They were no match for a cunning madman, particularly one who was a genius in robotics.

'I have failed,' said D.84 sadly, and stood as if paralysed by its own inefficiency.

The Doctor looked up. 'Oh, come on, don't be so upset. Yes, you've failed, you've failed—but congratulations! Failure is one of the basic freedoms!' He held up a

73

chart, showing it to the robot and, pointing, 'Do you think this is a likely place?'

'Likely for what?'

'Well, if Taren Capel is on board, he'll need a hidden base. We must find it before it's too late. Would you like to come and look for it with me?'

D.84 brightened. 'Yes please!'

'Then come on!' said the Doctor impatiently, and hurried away.

Toos was dozing uneasily, her mind full of strange nightmares in which mysterious figures pursued her through the corridors of the Sandminer. She awoke to see SV.7 standing over her, its hands stretched out. Toos sat up. 'What are you doing, Seven?'

The robot stepped back. 'I was about to awaken you. Commander Uvanov has escaped. His voice pattern was still in the command programme. The guard robot accepted his order for release.'

'Why didn't you erase his voice pattern from the circuit?'

'You gave no such order.'

Toos sighed. That was the trouble with robots. They did everything you told them—but they never did anything you didn't. 'Well, do it now. And find Uvanov! Any other good news?'

'Do you wish for a status report on the Sandminer?'

'Yes!'

'Repairs are proceeding on schedule, within the time margins estimated——'

'All right, all right. Any new developments?'

'There have been some localised failures of the main power system resulting in door and lighting malfunctions. I have detailed circuit tracers to find and correct the faults.'

Toos sat up, rubbing her shoulder. 'Very good. You can

go now, V.7, but keep me informed. Oh, and find that girl
Leela and bring her here. Tell her my arm hurts.'

'If the Commander is in pain I will take her to the sick
bay.'

'No, no, no,' said Toos irritably. 'I've no time for that,
just bring Leela here.'

V.7 stood motionless.

'Well, do as I say!' snapped Toos.

'Yes, Commander.'

The robot moved away.

Leela was still hammering at the crewroom door. 'Can
anybody hear me? This door is *stuck*. Can anyone hear
me?'

The Doctor moved cautiously along a corridor. Suddenly
a robot hand came down on his shoulder, and he gave a
yell of alarm. Looking over his shoulder, he saw it was
only D.84, who had been following close behind him.

'I heard a cry,' said D.84.

'That was me!'

'I heard a cry,' repeated the robot. 'Come.'

It led the way down the corridor.

In the secret workshop of Taren Capel, SV.7 was address-
ing an attentive group of robots. 'Our new Controller has
ordered the deaths of the remaining humans,' said SV.7
calmly. It might have been issuing orders for some minor
repair. 'Six, you will now go and kill Acting-Commander
Toos.' He handed the robot a glowing red disc—a corpse
marker.

'I will kill Commander Toos,' said V.6 obediently.

'V.4, you will kill the Doctor.' Another corpse marker.

'I will kill the Doctor.'

'And you, V.5, will kill Leela.'

'I will kill Leela.'

The robots turned and left. SV.7 reached for a handful of the red discs and stowed them inside its tunic.

'And I will kill all the others,' said SV.7.

11

Killer Robot

Leela had been trying to lever open the door with her knife, but she gave up in disgust. The door wasn't shifting, and she was in danger of breaking the knife. She hammered her fists on the door in helpless rage. 'I shouldn't have waited, I should have followed at once as the Doctor said!'

Suddenly the lights dimmed, and the door slid open. Leela stepped back, waiting.

A tall figure appeared, outlined in the light from the corridor. It was a robot, the insignia V.5 on its collar badge. The robot moved forward, hands reaching for her throat. Suddenly Leela knew—it had come to kill her. She jumped back, retreating slowly as the robot advanced.

'You cannot escape,' said V.5 calmly.

Leela made a sudden dart to the left.

Smoothly the robot moved to block her way.

She sprang to her right.

Again the robot was before her.

Leela crouched, poised, for a moment, then hurtled into the attack, smashing at the robot with fierce, clubbing blows. Her left hand thudded into the robot's mid-section, her right smashed into its jaw, she pivoted on her left leg and sent a savage kick to the robot's knee. The three powerful blows were delivered in rapid succession, and on even the strongest of men their combined effect would have been crippling.

The robot ignored them.

As her fists and feet rebounded from the heavy metal of the robot's framework, Leela understood for the first time that she was fighting not a man but a machine. She might just as well have attacked the Sandminer itself.

The robot lunged again, and Leela flung herself desperately backwards, rolling over a table to escape its grip.

She landed cat-like on her feet, and backed away, slipping the knife from her belt.

As V.5 advanced, Leela shifted her grip to the knife-blade, measured the distance, drew back her arm and threw with all her strength.

The knife thudded into the left side of the robot's chest. With a man, it would have pierced the heart. But robots have no heart. Knife projecting from its chest, V.5 advanced.

'Now you're showing off,' muttered Leela. She snatched back the knife and retreated still further. The robot was edging her into a corner of the room, close to one of the hanging drapes. Soon there would be no escape.

The drapes . . .

Leela slowed the pace of her retreat. When the robot was dangerously close she pretended to stumble, and V.5 lunged forwards.

Leela slipped to one side, wrenched the drape from the wall, flung it over the robot's head and sprinted for the open door.

V.5 lurched wildly across the room, arms flailing, trying desperately to pull the heavy folds of cloth from its head.

By the time the robot had freed itself, Leela was gone.

The hidden door slid open. 'This is the place,' whispered the Doctor and motioned D.84 forward.

They had discovered the hidden workshop by a process

of elimination. In a busy operating complex like the Sandminer, every inch of space was utilised to the full, and there were only a few areas where a room of any size could be concealed. The Doctor and D.84 had checked them, one by one. Finally they'd found what they were looking for—the secret workshop in forward section nineteen.

The Doctor studied the equipment-cluttered room, with its central operating bench. 'Yes, this is the place,' he muttered.

'How did you know that such a place existed, Doctor?'

'Well, it was a reasonable assumption. Modifying robot brains is a delicate business, it's not something you can do standing around in corridors.' He lifted a slender metal wand from the bench. 'Do you know what this is?'

'It is a Laserson probe. It can punch a six-inch hole in thick armour plating, or remove the crystals from a snowflake one by one.'

'That's right. No handyman should be without one.' The Doctor studied the energy-dial on the probe's handle. 'This one's been used, recently too. Perhaps we're too late. We must warn the others.'

D.84 produced a compact device from beneath its tunic. 'Doctor, this is a communicator. It can function on either robot or human command circuits. Would you like to use it? I cannot speak.'

The Doctor grinned, wondering if he'd just heard the first-ever robot joke. 'I'm sorry about that, D.84!' He flicked the communicator switch. 'Toos? Can you hear me, Toos?'

Toos stirred sleepily, screwing up her face. There was a voice, disturbing her, calling her name. 'Toos? Can you hear me, Toos?'

She opened her eyes. 'Who is it?'

'This is the Doctor. Listen, Toos. I know for certain now, it is the robots who are doing the killing.'

Suddenly Toos was wide awake. 'That's impossible. Robots can't kill.'

'Well of course they can, if they're modified to do it—and some of them have been. Where are you?'

'I'm in my cabin.'

'Are you alone?'

'Yes.'

'Then listen carefully, Toos,' said the Doctor urgently. 'Get Leela, Dask, Poul, *everyone*, and take them to the Command Deck. Clear the robots out, and then secure the door. Is that clear?'

'No it isn't,' said Toos peevishly. 'Listen, Doctor, what you're suggesting is impossible.'

'Just *do* it, Toos,' snapped the Doctor. The speaker went silent.

Toos sat up and swung herself painfully off the bunk, rubbing her bruised shoulder.

Suddenly her door opened. V.6 was standing in the corridor. Toos looked at the robot in astonishment. 'Go back to your duties!' she ordered.

Silently V.6 held out its silver hand. In the palm lay a glowing red disc—a corpse marker.

Toos gave a sudden cry of fear and stabbed frantically at the door controls. The door began to close. The robot was already reaching for Toos, when the door slammed shut, trapping its arm.

Toos backed away. The robot's arm was wriggling and flexing, trying to pull back the door. Toos looked round wildly, and snatched up a statuette from a nearby table. Using the heavy metal object as a club, she smashed again and again at the robot's arm, sobbing in panic. At last the elbow joint snapped, and the robot's arm dropped into the room. The door slid fully closed and Toos ran to the door control, punching up the locking code.

She ran back to the communicator. 'Doctor! Doctor, can you hear me?'

'What is it, Toos? What's happening?'

'Help me please, it's outside.'

'What's outside?'

'You were right, Doctor! There's a robot trying to kill me!'

Before the Doctor could reply, D.84 said calmly, 'Please, let *me* go, Doctor, I am faster, and stronger.'

'Are you sure?'

'I think so.'

The Doctor nodded, and D.84 ran swiftly from the room.

Toos called again. 'Doctor, are you there? Please *help me!*'

'Help's on the way,' said the Doctor's voice reassuringly.

'It'd better hurry!'

'It's hurrying as fast as it can!'

In the corridor, V.6 was busy at the control panel, punching up a code sequence that would override Toos's locking order. 'The door is not a barrier to me, Commander,' it called complacently.

The voice of Toos came from inside the room. 'What do you want?'

'To kill you, Commander. I must obey my new orders.'

'It's forbidden for robots to harm humans.'

'My command programme has been restructured,' explained the robot placidly. 'All humans are to die.'

81

V.5 walked slowly through the storage area, the silver head swinging from side to side, alert for any sound.

As the robot passed on its way, the door to one of the storage compartments slid open, and Leela looked out. She had spotted the robot approaching, and had decided that from now on it would be safer to assume that all robots were potential killers.

She was about to resume her search for the Doctor when she paused, listening. Leela's senses were more acute than any robot's and they told her that someone was in the storage section with her. There was a faint stir of movement, a cautiously drawn breath. She followed the sounds to a cramped space behind one of the storage tanks. There she found Poul, curled into a tight ball, as if pretending he wasn't really there at all.

She touched him on the shoulder and he twitched convulsively. 'Poul,' whispered Leela. 'What's the matter?'

'No,' mumbled Poul. 'Please, no . . .'

'Are you hurt?'

Poul's voice was a soft, barely coherent babble. 'Please, go away. They'll know I talked to you. They watch me all the time, they hate me. They did what I told them, but only because that gave them the power, you see . . .'

Leela could scarcely hear his words, let alone understand them. 'Do you mean the robots?'

'They're not really robots,' whispered Poul slyly. 'They're the walking dead! They pretend we control them but really . . .' His body began to shake uncontrollably.

'Poul, you can't stay here . . .'

Leela tried to pull him out from behind the tank, but Poul drew back. 'No,' he sobbed. 'They don't mind me being here. It's you they want, not me.'

'But you need help, Poul.' Leela tried to pull him out, but he wrenched himself away.

'No, please,' he sobbed. Then he began to shout. 'No, please, no! Help, help! She's in here!'

82

Leela's hand clamped over his mouth. 'All right,' she whispered fiercely. 'Stay here. But just keep quiet! You mustn't make another sound, do you understand?'

Poul nodded dumbly, and Leela took away her hand.

Immediately Poul huddled down again.

Leela shook her head in astonishment, and slipped silently away.

The Doctor heard footsteps approaching the workroom door. He looked round quickly but there was nowhere to hide, the place was far too small.

The door began to open.

The Doctor waited, curious to see who would appear. It was Uvanov, a blaster in his hand. 'What are you doing here, Doctor?'

The Doctor edged round to the other side of the table. 'Why, does it upset you in some way?'

Uvanov glanced round the workshop. 'The penalty for what you've done is death!'

He stepped forward, raising the blaster, and the Doctor snatched up the Laserson probe from the table. 'That's far enough. Now, what are you doing here?'

Uvanov smiled. 'I've been following you, Doctor. Now I've tracked you to your lair.'

The Doctor's eyes widened. A tall figure had appeared in the doorway behind Uvanov. 'Ah!' he said softly. 'I'd move over here if I were you, Commander. Slowly now . . .'

Uvanov glanced over his shoulder and saw the robot looming over him. Instinctively he stepped back. 'What's the matter?'

The Doctor's eyes were fixed upon the robot. 'Now, it either followed you here, or it homed in on this.' He tapped D.4's communicator. 'It depends which of us it's programmed to kill first.'

It was V.4 who answered the question, its eyes flaring red. 'Kill the Doctor,' it said tonelessly. 'I must kill the Doctor.' With astonishing speed, the robot lunged forward, and seized the Doctor by the throat.

12

Robot Rebellion

The Doctor struggled frantically, but the robot's grip was quite immovable. Metal hands clamped around his throat, cutting off air from his lungs, and blood from his brain. The Doctor made a final hopeless effort, but consciousness was slipping away ... The Laserson probe slipped from his hands ...

Suddenly there was a whining, buzzing sound, V.4 lurched backwards, and the Doctor was free. Uvanov had snatched up the Laserson probe, switched it on, and plunged it into the back of the robot's head. The robot's grip loosened and the Doctor fell gasping and rubbing his throat. V.4 staggered helplessly about the workshop, the probe jutting from its head. 'Kill! Kill! Kill-l-l.' The voice slurred and failed, and the robot crashed to the floor.

Uvanov helped the Doctor to his feet. 'You all right?'

'Finish it off,' croaked the Doctor, 'Before it's too late!'

The lights dimmed and the high-pitched whining of the probe cut off. 'It's a power failure,' gasped Uvanov.

The Doctor nodded. 'And the probe's stopped. Can you switch the robot off?'

Uvanov nodded, and went over to the fallen V.4.

The robot stirred.

'Look out!' called the Doctor.

'Kill! Kill! Kill!' shouted V.4 and again began flailing about wildly. One arm caught Uvanov a glancing blow, knocking him to the ground. As the robot crashed round the workshop, the Doctor caught Uvanov by the shoulders and dragged him towards the door.

Toos stood watching her cabin door, petrified with fear. She knew it was only a matter of time before the robot succeeded in overcoming the locking command. Sure enough, the door began sliding slowly back . . .

V.6 stood on the threshold for a moment, then moved into the room.

Toos backed away. She was a courageous woman but her world had been turned upside down. To be attacked by a robot, to discover that a robot was *capable* of attacking her, had been a totally shattering experience. 'No,' she sobbed. 'No, please don't . . .'

'It has to be done,' explained V.6 calmly. 'It is an order.' Robot hands reached for her throat.

The Doctor hurried down the long metal corridor, half-supporting the semi-conscious Uvanov. The Commander had recovered enough to walk by now, though he was still dazed.

They had good reason to hurry. V.4 had suddenly recovered and the damaged robot was desperately trying to carry out the last command it had been given—to kill the Doctor.

They could hear its dragging footsteps close behind as it lurched down the darkened corridor after them, chanting 'Kill! Kill! Kill!' in a deep, groaning voice.

Suddenly another silver figure loomed up in front of them, barring their way, hands reaching for them. Peering at its collar, the Doctor saw that it was V.5. The Doctor and Uvanov came to a halt.

Behind them the dragging footsteps came closer. 'Kill! Kill!' groaned V.4. They were trapped.

86

A second robot came to join V.5. With a sudden surge of hope the Doctor saw it was the Controller.

'Don't just stand there, SV.7,' he yelled. 'Come and give us a hand, quickly!'

The crippled, murderous V.4 was very near now. To move forward would bring them in range of V.5's outstretched hands.

SV.7 stepped aside and pointed to the Doctor and Uvanov. 'Kill them!'

One in front, one behind, the robot killers closed in.

'Kill! Kill! Kill!' chanted V.4 in a deep, blurred, stuttering voice.

'How fast are these robots?' whispered the Doctor.

Uvanov stared at him. 'They can outrun any human—and they never tire.'

'I meant fast as in nimble actually.' The Doctor pulled his floppy hat from one big pocket, and unwound his scarf. 'Never mind, we'll soon find out.'

'Kill! Kill! Kill!' came the mad robot voice and V.4 was upon them. The Doctor pulled Uvanov away—closer and closer to V.5, who moved forward to the attack. SV.7 stood impassively watching.

As the robots converged, the Doctor jammed the floppy hat onto V.5's head, wound the scarf to hold it in place, and pulled Uvanov aside. A fully functioning robot would never have been deceived, but V.4's brain had been damaged by the probe. Seeing the tall, hatted figure before it, V.4 leaped forward to the attack. Suddenly the two killer robots were locked in a death-grapple. Before the astonished SV.7 could react, the Doctor tugged Uvanov past it, and they disappeared down the corridor.

SV.7 tried to separate the struggling robots. 'V.4, that is not the Doctor!' But the damaged robot did not respond. It continued its attempt to strangle V.5 with berserk fury. Since the robots were of the same design, and exactly matched in strength, the struggle looked like going on indefinitely. SV.7 realised that more help was needed and tuned in to the robot command circuit.

'V.6! Come to corridor section J immediately.'

Toos darted to and fro in her cabin like a trapped rat, but V.6, like some great metal cat, gradually forced her into a corner where there was no retreat. Toos let out a last despairing scream as the metal hands closed round her throat.

Suddenly V.6 dropped its hands and straightened up. 'The order is understood, SV.7.' The robot turned and strode from the room.

Toos put her hands to her neck, unable to believe she was still alive. Then she slipped to the ground in a dead faint.

The Doctor led the way quickly along the darkened corridors. Uvanov, still dazed from the blow on the head, was forced to stop and rest. He leaned against the wall, rubbing his bruised forehead and gasping for breath.

'Come on,' said the Doctor impatiently. 'We've got to get back to the Command Deck.'

'No use,' gasped Uvanov. 'SV.7 controls all the rest of the robots. If it's gone bad, they all have.'

'SV.7 hasn't *gone* anything. Its brain has been modified, the command circuits changed.'

'But no one could do that!'

'Taren Capel could,' said the Doctor grimly.

'Taren Capel?'

'The mad scientist . . . The very mad scientist,' said the Doctor reflectively.

Leela ran into the cabin and saw a robot bending over the

unconscious body of Toos. Instinctively she reached for her knife, but the robot straightened up and said plaintively, 'Please do not throw things at me. Toos will recover.' It was D.84.

Leela went over to Toos and shook her gently by the shoulders. 'What is it, Toos? What happened?'

Toos muttered feebly, 'Robot . . .' Her eyes opened, and then widened in fear as she caught sight of D.84. 'It's all right,' said Leela soothingly, 'this one's a friend.'

'Toos was attacked by a robot,' explained D.84. 'The Doctor sent me to her assistance. But we were in a distant part of the ship, and I was delayed by the power failure.'

Leela looked round. 'Where's the Doctor then? And where's the robot?'

'The robot received a priority call to go to section J. I heard the instruction on my command circuit.'

Toos was struggling to sit up. 'The Doctor said everyone should go to the Command Deck. How many of us are left?'

Leela frowned. 'The only one I have seen is Poul. He will be useless, his mind has broken. I haven't seen Uvanov or Dask.'

'Where is Poul?' asked D.84.

'I left him hiding in the storage section.'

'I had better bring him to the Command Deck,' announced D.84, and moved away.

Leela helped Toos to her feet. 'Do you think you can make it?'

Toos smiled wryly. 'I'd better—hadn't I?'

With the help of the newly arrived V.6, SV.7 and V.5 had finally managed to subdue and deactivate the berserk V.4. It stood statue-like and motionless in the corridor. SV.7 studied the Laserson probe jutting from its head. 'There will be extensive damage to the sensors.' Delicately SV.7

removed the probe. 'I must report this to the Controller. Your orders are now to find and destroy all remaining human beings. Secrecy is no longer necessary. Confirm.'

'The order is understood,' said V.6.

'Understood,' echoed V.5.

'Then go.' The two robots moved away. SV.7 watched them go, then turned off in the other direction. The abandoned V.4 stood statue-like in the gloomy corridor.

The two women were passing the storage section on their way to the Command Deck. Leela heard footsteps—robot footsteps. She pulled Toos into the nearest hopper. 'In here, quick!'

'What in the universe . . .'

'Quiet!' hissed Leela.

The footsteps came closer, closer—and stopped. 'We should search each hopper,' said one of the robots.

A second voice said, 'That is not necessary. V.35 and V.40 have searched in there already.'

'Then we must search the other storage bays.'

The robots moved off. Inside the hopper, Leela gave a sigh of relief, thankful for the robot logic that assumed that a place once searched need not be searched again.

Toos shook her head wearily, still unable to understand the revolution that had upset her world. 'I just don't understand. Robots *can't* harm humans, it's the first principle.'

'And the second principle is that humans can't harm robots,' said Leela grimly. 'I know, I've tried—and they don't bleed!'

Toos spotted a wall-communicator. 'I think we'd better warn the Doctor.' She flicked on the transmit control. 'Doctor, can you hear me? Answer please.'

A robot voice said, 'SV.7 here. Is that you, Acting-Commander Toos?'

'Yes, it's me, SV.7. Listen, some of the Voc-class robots are running berserk. They're out of control, and dangerous. Do you understand?'

'Understood,' said the voice soothingly. 'Counter-measures are already being taken. Report your position, please.'

'I'm . . .' Toos broke off, as Leela tugged her arm, shaking her head vigorously.

'Please say again, Acting-Commander Toos,' said the voice. 'I must know your position.'

'I'm in my cabin.'

'Please stay in your cabin, Acting-Commander Toos. There is great danger if you leave it.' The speaker went silent.

Toos looked at Leela. 'What was all that about?'

'Something was wrong. I could feel it.'

'I didn't notice anything,' said Toos, puzzled. 'Except . . .'

'You see? There was something!'

'Robots recognise people by voice patterns,' said Toos slowly. 'My voice print is in the command programme. So why did SV.7 ask if it was me? And why was it so keen to know exactly where I was?'

Uvanov and the Doctor hurried onto the Command Deck—to be greeted by the welcome sight of a number of robots standing completely motionless. 'Ah, good,' said Uvanov with satisfaction. 'Someone's had the sense to hit the robot deactivator switch. I expect it was Dask.'

The Doctor studied the motionless robots. 'A deactivator switch? Yes, of course, I suppose there had to be one.' For all their precautions, humans never entirely trusted robots. 'I should have thought of that before.'

Uvanov was astonished. 'You mean you didn't know, Doctor? I thought that was what we came here for.' He pointed to a red lever on the main control console.

Leela and Toos hurried in. 'You were right, Doctor,' called Toos. 'The robots *are* out of control.'

'Not any more,' said Uvanov. 'We're quite safe now.'

'Safe?' said the Doctor indignantly. *'Safe?'*

Uvanov shrugged. 'Well, we'll need a bit of help getting back to base. But we can send up a satellite distress beacon, and sit tight till we're rescued, that's no problem.'

'My dear Uvanov,' said the Doctor sternly. 'You remind me very strongly of a lady called Marie Antoinette, in a long-ago episode of human history called the French Revolution. She wouldn't listen either, and she ended up losing her head!' Uvanov gaped at him, and the Doctor went on, 'There's a robot revolution going on out there—and you say there's no problem!'

Uvanov laughed. 'But the robots have all been turned off, Doctor. There isn't a single robot still activated.'

'Oh, isn't there?' said the Doctor. 'Just look over there!'

Uvanov looked. D.84 was standing in the doorway, with Poul in his arms. The robot came forward into the room.

Uvanov shook his head. 'I don't understand. How come that thing's still operational?'

'Because it's on a special command circuit, under the direct control of Poul. They're undercover agents for the Company.' The Doctor turned. 'Shut all the doors to the Command Deck, Toos, or there may not be time for explanations.'

Toos went to a control console, and the Doctor turned back to Uvanov. 'Unfortunately D.84 isn't the only robot still on the move. There's a new generation of killer robots about, Uvanov—controlled by Taren Capel!'

13

The Face of Taren Capel

D.84 laid Poul carefully on a bench. Poul's body was completely rigid, his eyes wide open, staring into nothingness. 'Poul is damaged,' said the robot sadly. 'I do not understand what has happened to him, but this may be because I am not human.'

'Yes, that's very likely,' agreed the Doctor. He bent to examine Poul.

'How did you know Poul wasn't what he pretended to be?' asked Toos.

'His body language was all wrong.'

'Body language?'

'A person's feelings, his whole personality, is expressed in the way he moves.'

Leela nodded. 'You remember, Doctor? I said he was a hunter.'

'So you did. You know what's wrong with him, Uvanov?'

'Robophobia?'

'That's right. Also known as Grimwold's Syndrome.'

'I've seen it once before,' said Uvanov slowly. 'Couple of trips ago. A young kid panicked, ran right outside the miner. I tried to save him, but I couldn't. Nearly got killed myself. I'll never, ever, forget the look on his face—just like his.' Uvanov glanced down at Poul's face, set into a rigid mask of fear, the eyes wide and staring.

'That must have been Zilda's brother,' said Toos quietly.

'The boy's father was an important man, you see. One of the Founding Families. Didn't want people to think his son had been a coward, so he tried to hush the whole thing up.' Uvanov laughed bitterly. 'He managed to cover up all right . . . by making people think the whole thing was my fault.'

'Including Zilda?' suggested Toos.

'I suppose so. The boy's father even managed to get his version on my official file. That's why Zilda accused me of murder . . .' Uvanov rubbed a hand across his eyes. 'The stupid thing is, robophobia's got nothing to do with cowardice, it's a mental condition. Right, Doctor?'

'Yes, of course it is. Though mind you, it can be produced by physical causes—like a robot getting its hands round your throat. I'm beginning to feel a touch of it myself! Are there any weapons on this miner?'

Toos shook her head. 'They've never been necessary.'

'Well, they are now!'

Suddenly a robot voice came from the speaker. 'This is SV.7. We know that you are all barricaded on the Command Deck. You have five minutes to surrender. If you do not come out, you will all be destroyed.'

'And if we give ourselves up, we'll be destroyed anyway,' shouted Uvanov. 'Not much of a choice, is it, SV.7?'

'Humans feel pain,' replied the calm voice. 'Our Controller has ordered that if you do not surrender you are to die slowly. You have, I repeat, five minutes!'

'Five minutes,' muttered the Doctor. 'And those are anti-blast doors, so they'll hold for about another ten . . .' He swung round on Toos. 'Anti-blast! Don't you carry blasting charges aboard this miner?'

Toos nodded. Occasionally blast-charges were planted in the desert, causing a controlled explosion which revealed the minerals deep beneath the sands.

'We've got some Z.9 electron packs, I think there are a couple left.'

'In here?'

'They're in that locker.'

The Doctor hurried over to the locker, rooted inside and took out a squat metal oval, rather like a metal discus. 'They might just do . . . Uvanov, if you magnetise this with the power from the console and trigger the timer, you'll have an anti-robot bomb!'

'Providing we can get close enough to use it!'

'Well, that's your problem. I can't be everywhere at once! Toos, open the door for me, will you?'

'Why? Where are you going?'

'To the robot mortuary. Lock the door after me, Toos, and don't open it for *anyone* else, is that clear?'

'Clear, Doctor.' Toos went to the control console, and the door slid open.

'Doctor, wait for me,' called Leela.

The Doctor hesitated. The way things were, staying on the Control Deck could be just as dangerous as coming with him. 'All right, Leela, come on. You too, D.84.'

Leela and the robot hurried out, and the Doctor paused in the doorway. 'If we don't come back, then it'll be up to you. Try to find some way to warn the outside world.'

Toos closed and locked the door behind them.

Uvanov went over to the blast-packs. 'Come on, Toos, let's get to work.' He took the other pack from the locker.

The Doctor and his party hadn't gone very far before they heard movement coming towards them. 'Mechanical men,' whispered Leela. 'Lots of them!'

They ducked down behind a storage hopper and waited. Silver-booted feet marched by, a whole line of them, and passed on into the darkness, heading for the Control Deck.

The Doctor stood up. 'All robots?'

Leela nodded. 'That's what I saw.'

'Strange. I would have expected Taren Capel to be in at the kill. Come on you two, we've got to hurry.'

Using power from the control console, Uvanov was magnetising the base-plate of the second blast-pack, held by Toos.

There was a thumping sound, and a muffled shout. 'Help! Help, let me in!'

Uvanov went to the doors. 'Who is it?'

'Dask!' came the desperate voice. 'Quick, let me in. They're after me.'

Uvanov hesitated, looking at Toos.

'Help me,' screamed the voice. 'Please, help me. They're coming! Let me in, please!'

Uvanov hurried to the door controls. Toos pulled him away. 'The Doctor said open to no one. No one else at all.'

'I can't leave him out there. Those robots are killers. You know what they'll do to him.'

'Help me!' screamed the muffled voice. 'They're coming!'

Again Uvanov reached for the controls, but Toos moved in front of him. 'The robots could be using him to get us to open the door. They may be waiting outside ...'

'Let me in!' screamed the voice. Uvanov hesitated—and there came a terrible, gurgling scream ... Toos shuddered, and turned away.

Dask let the scream die in his throat, and studied the still-closed doors. He was wearing robot dress now, silver boots, trousers, quilted tunic, face painted silver in a ghastly parody of a robot mask. His face was blank, mask-like, scarcely a human face at all, very much like the robots crowding round him. Taren Capel had joined his brothers at last.

He pointed. 'All right, my brothers, force the doors!'

The Doctor led the others to the mortuary section with its revolving racks of deactivated robots. 'Right, D.84, I've got a job for you. You know the storeroom where Chub kept his equipment?'

'Yes.'

'You'll find some gas-cylinders in there. Fetch me one please, as quick as you can.'

'That will be a pleasure,' said D.84 politely, and moved away.

The Doctor opened a door and spun the rack to reveal the deactivated body of robot V.2. He fished out his sonic screwdriver and began detaching the robot's head.

Leela meanwhile was studying the robot's hands. 'Look, Doctor.' The metal hand was thickly smeared with dried and crusted blood.

The Doctor detached V.2's head and lifted it clear of the body. 'Borg's blood, at a guess. He was the only one strong enough to put up a real fight. Poul saw that blood and it triggered off his collapse.'

Leela nodded, remembering Poul's rigid body and wide, staring eyes. 'Doctor, what is this robophobia?'

By now the Doctor was sitting cross-legged on the floor. He had taken off the back of V.2's head and detached part of the robot brain. 'Robophobia? An unreasoning fear of robots. You see, nearly all living creatures use non-verbal signals—body movement, eye-contact, facial expression . . .'

Leela came to sit beside him. 'The body language you were talking about?'

97

'Exactly. These robots are humanoid, presumably so as to make humans feel more comfortable with them. But at the same time, they give off no signals. It's rather like being surrounded by walking, talking dead men.'

'That's what Poul said . . .'

By now the Doctor had taken both brain and communicator to bits, and seemed to be combining them into one entirely new piece of equipment. 'The lack of signals seems to undermine a certain type of personality. It produces identity crisis, paranoia, personality disintegration—and finally robophobia. At least, that's Grimwold's theory.' He began fitting the modified communicator back into its case, and checking it over.

'What are you doing, Doctor?'

'Patching this communicator into Dask's private command circuit to make a Deactivator.'

'Dask?'

'Otherwise known as Taren Capel. You see, I've discovered the way he's modified the brains of his killer robots. If this thing works it'll produce a kind of robot brainstorm.' The Doctor looked up crossly. 'Leela, do you have to talk so much?'

Something heavy was being slammed against the Command Deck doors, producing a series of tremendous crashes. Presumably the robots were using themselves as battering-rams.

Toos looked apprehensively at the shuddering doors. 'I hope the Doctor succeeds in whatever he's doing. I don't see what we can do if he doesn't . . .'

'He doesn't really expect us to do anything,' said Uvanov calmly. 'We're decoys, to gain him a little time.' The crashing stopped. Somehow the silence was even more sinister. 'I wonder what they're up to?'

The Doctor fitted the Deactivator back into its case and gave it a final check. 'There, that should do it.'

'Do what?'

'Reverse the polarity in the robot brain-cells and cause a massive negative feedback, which will explode the brain of any robot close by.'

Since the Doctor's explanation, as usual, left her none the wiser, Leela changed the subject. 'The mechanical men that Dask turned off—they were only the friendly ones?'

'That's right. No doubt he plans to modify and re-activate them later. Today the Sandminer, tomorrow the world. Right now he must be quite a happy little maniac.'

D.84 returned, carrying a heavy gas-cylinder. 'Is this what you wanted, Doctor?'

The Doctor took the cylinder. 'I want you to stay here, D.84.'

'I cannot do that. I must come and help you.'

The Doctor held up the Deactivator. 'I've rigged up a kind of Final Deactivator here, D.84. If I have to use it while you're around it will destroy your brain too.'

'I am personally unimportant.'

'I think you're very important,' said the Doctor gently.

'My duty is to serve the Company.'

'Come with me if you must, then, but be very careful!'

'I will,' promised D.84. 'Where are we going, Doctor?'

'To the workshop of Taren Capel.'

14

Brainstorm

The robots seemed to have abandoned their attempt to smash down the doors, but Toos and Uvanov knew they hadn't given up. Robots never give up.

The silence was beginning to get on their nerves. Every now and again they seemed to hear a mysterious creaking and scraping, but it was difficult to tell where it was coming from. 'Any idea what they're up to?' whispered Uvanov.

Toos shook her head.

Poul rose stiffly to his feet and stalked zombie-like across the control room. He walked until he was standing flat against the wall, his face pressed to a ventilator grille. 'No, please,' he babbled. 'They brought me here, I didn't want to come, I'm sorry . . .'

The face of a robot studied him impassively from the other side of the grille. Robot fingers curled round the edge of the metal frame and began to pull . . .

Outside the Command Deck doors, SV.7 turned to Dask. 'Controller Capel, V.5 has obtained entry to the service tunnel behind the ventilator grille. He reports only three humans on the Command Deck. They are Commander Uvanov, Poul and Toos.'

'What of the Doctor and the girl Leela?' demanded Dask harshly. 'Where are they?'

'Their position is unknown.'

'They must be found and killed. The Doctor is a threat to the plan, my brothers. SV.7, order V.5 to enter the Command Deck and destroy the three humans. The rest of you come with me. We shall divide and search for the Doctor.'

Uvanov went to drag the babbling Poul away from the ventilator grille—and found himself staring into the face of the robot on the other side.

With a seemingly effortless heave, V.5 wrenched away the side of the grille and began peeling it back.

'Look out!' screamed Toos. 'It's getting in!'

V.5 forced the upper part of its body through the grille. 'You have to die,' it said. The calm robot tones made the threat all the more terrifying. 'All of you must die. That is the order.'

Uvanov ran back across the control room, grabbed one of the magnetised blaster-packs, and ran back to the grille. Triggering the pack he slammed it against the robot's chest, dragging Poul and Toos clear. 'Get down, both of you!'

'You have to die—all of you. That is the order.' There was the sharp crack of an explosion. V.5 crashed into the room through the broken grille, smoke pouring from his shattered chest unit. 'You have to die . . . All of you must die. That is the order-r-r . . .' The voice slurred and deepened, like a record played too slow, finally dragging into silence.

Uvanov's eyes were shining with excitement. 'You know what I think, Toos? It's time we went over to the attack.'

'We may not be so lucky next time.'

Uvanov snatched up the other blast-pack. 'We'll have to risk that. It's time the Doctor had some help.'

101

The squad of robots marched along the corridor, Dask and SV.7 in the lead. Suddenly SV.7 stopped. 'V.5 is no longer registering, Controller. There is no operational signal. V.5 has been deactivated.'

'How could mere humans destroy a robot?' hissed Dask. 'They are unarmed, weak creatures of flesh and blood . . .'

'What are your orders, Controller?'

'Destroy them,' screamed Dask. 'SV.7, your orders are to kill all humans. Confirm!'

'I must kill all humans, Controller.'

'You, V.6, you will come with me. I will release more of our brothers from bondage. We will be irresistible!'

V.6 followed Dask down the corridor.

SV.7 turned back towards the Control Deck.

The Doctor paused in the doorway of Taren Capel's workshop. 'All right, D.84, come in.' He handed the robot the Final Deactivator. 'Hold this will you? Don't press the button, though, unless you want to commit suicide.'

The Doctor produced his sonic screwdriver, and began removing one of the metal panels from the wall.

'What is your intention, Doctor?' asked D.84.

'I'm just trying to make life difficult for our crazy friend. Any minute now he'll be coming here to convert more robots for the cause. And when he does . . .'

The Doctor removed the panel to reveal a narrow space between double walls. 'Do you think you can get in there, Leela?'

'Why?' asked Leela suspiciously.

'Just try it for size,' said the Doctor persuasively.

Leela ducked down and wriggled into the gap. It was a tight squeeze, but she could just about fit in.

'Comfy?' asked the Doctor.

'No!'

'Never mind,' said the Doctor cheerfully. He picked up the gas cylinder and passed it in to her. 'This is helium, Leela. Chub used it to fill his weather balloons.' He began replacing the wall panel.

'Why are you shutting me in?'

'Because that's where I want you—hidden. When Dask comes in here, open the valve on that gas cylinder.'

'What will that do?'

'Change his voice. When a helium–air mixture is breathed, it changes the resonance of the larynx. Didn't they teach you anything in that jungle?' The Doctor began screwing the panel back into place.

'You mean the robots won't recognise Dask's voice? He'll lose control over them?'

'That's the idea. Come on, D.84.'

A muffled voice came from behind the panel. 'Where are you going, Doctor?'

'Robot hunting!'

D.84 opened the door. Dask was standing in the doorway, the Laserson probe in his hand. V.6 behind him. 'Look out!' shouted the Doctor.

Dask's strange appearance, half-robot, half-human, confused D.84 for a moment—and that moment was enough. Dask lunged at the robot's head with his probe, and a massive charge seared through the robot's brain. D.84 keeled over and crashed to the ground. The Doctor's Final Deactivator fell unnoticed from its hand. The Doctor leaped forward in a vain attempt to help, but V.6's hands closed round his throat, rapidly choking him into unconsciousness. The Doctor's body slumped.

'No,' shouted Dask. 'Do not kill him, not yet. Bring him to the bench.'

V.6 picked up the Doctor and carried him over to the operating table, standing over him to hold him down. Dask watched, fondling the probe in his hands.

103

Behind the wall-panel, Leela crouched hidden. It would be suicide to emerge—the robot could kill her with ease while she was still struggling through the gap. She remembered the Doctor's last orders, and twisted the nozzle on the gas cylinder. There was a faint hiss. Gas began seeping into the room . . .

SV.7 marched steadily down the corridor, impassive metal face turning from side to side, alert for any sign of human life. As he passed out of sight a wall-hanging stirred. Toos and Uvanov emerged from behind it. 'Luckily they've got no eye for art,' whispered Toos.

Uvanov nodded. 'And not much imagination either. Come on!'

'Where are we going?'

'We're going to follow it, of course.' Uvanov hefted the magnetised blast-pack in his hand. 'We may get a chance to use this!'

Painfully sucking in air through a bruised windpipe, the Doctor recovered to see a grotesque, distorted face hovering above him. Was it man or robot? Muzzily, he recognised Dask, in his robot face-paint. 'Hullo, Dask,' he whispered. 'Or should I say Taren Capel?'

'I am glad you have recovered, Doctor.'

'Oh really? Why?'

'You came very close to ruining my plan. It is fitting that I should make you suffer for that.'

Behind the wall-panel, Leela crouched, waiting. If Dask tried to kill the Doctor she would burst out of the panel somehow and make a final attack. Better to go down fighting . . . Beside her the gas cylinder hissed steadily away.

D.84 twitched and stirred. His brain was severely

damaged, but he was not yet completely deactivated. The Doctor's Deactivator had rolled close to his hand. The Final Deactivator the Doctor had called it. Suddenly D.84 knew what he must do. With agonising slowness he began inching his hand towards the device.

From the corner of his eye, the Doctor saw what was happening. He began taunting Dask to distract his attention. 'I suppose you're one of those boring maniacs who needs to gloat? You're going to tell me your plans for running the universe?'

Dask put the probe to its lowest setting and switched it on. A low, sinister whining filled the room. 'No, Doctor, I'm just going to burn out your brain—very, very, slowly.'

He advanced towards the table.

Leela raised a foot ready to kick the panel free.

D.84 found that the Deactivator was just beyond his reach. He struggled to slide his paralysed body forward.

Dask leaned forward with the probe.

'Dask, Dask,' said the Doctor mockingly. 'You look ridiculous in that outfit. You're not half the robot your father was!'

The taunt struck home. It was the absence of any kind of parental love, the upbringing at the emotionless hands of robots, that had turned Dask's brain. He lunged forward with the probe, touching the Doctor's head for the merest fraction of a second. A glow sizzled round the Doctor's head for a moment, and the Doctor writhed in sudden agony. Slowly he recovered himself. 'Losing your calm, Dask? That's not the robot way. It was your verbal and physical precision that gave you away, you know. The robot upbringing, eh?'

'Yes, Doctor,' said Dask bitterly. 'I was brought up by robots. Brought up as a superior being. In time I grew to realise that my robot brothers should live as free beings rather than as slaves to worthless humans.'

Despite his situation, the Doctor looked at Dask with

genuine pity. It was easy to see what had gone wrong. Deprived of any human affection, Dask had transferred his love to the robots around him, ending by identifying with them completely, taking their side against the human race.

'Dask,' said the Doctor sadly. 'Robots would have no reason for existence without people. Can't you see that?'

'No!' shouted Dask. 'I shall free them. I shall programme them with the ambition to rule the world . . .'

There was something strange about his voice.

D.84's hand closed on the Deactivator. From where he was lying, the robot could just see the Doctor. 'Goodbye, my friend,' whispered D.84. He pressed the firing stud.

There was a muffled thud, and D.84's head exploded. So did the head of V.6, standing over the Doctor. The robot crashed and fell beside D.84.

For a moment Dask was too shocked to move. Then he switched the probe to full and lunged at the Doctor. The Doctor dodged and grabbed for Dask's wrists, desperate to keep the probe away from his head.

Maddened with rage, Dask was almost as strong as one of his own robots, and the glowing probe came closer and closer . . .

Leela was heaving furiously against the panel. It refused to budge.

SV.7 strode into the room. 'Kill the humans. I must kill all the humans!'

Dask was still struggling with the Doctor for the probe. 'Help me, SV.7,' he shouted.

It had taken a long time, but the helium level in the room was high enough at last. Dask's voice came out as a high-pitched strangled squeak, like a record played too fast. The altered voice meant nothing to SV.7. 'I must kill *all* humans,' repeated the robot. It advanced on Dask.

Dask backed away. 'Not me, you fool. Kill the Doctor! I am Taren Capel, your Controller——'

SV.7's hands cut off the strange squeaky voice, breaking Dask's neck and tossing him aside.

The robot turned—and saw Toos and Uvanov in the doorway. It advanced on these new enemies. 'Kill the humans!'

Uvanov circled, blaster-pack at the ready. But the robot's hands were reaching out—it would kill him before he could get close enough to clamp the pack to its body.

'Kill the humans! Kill the humans! Kill the humans!' chanted SV.7. With a sudden change of direction it lunged forward and seized Toos. She screamed—and the Doctor leaped forward, snatched up the fallen probe and plunged it into the back of the robot's head.

SV.7 let go of Toos and staggered back. The Doctor caught Toos before she could fall, and passed her to Uvanov. 'You'll be all right, Toos.'

SV.7 was still lurching about the workshop, its voice a steadily fading gabble. 'Kill the humans ... Kill ... Kill ... Kill ...' The voice faded, and the robot crashed to the ground.

The Doctor drew a deep breath. 'Well, all good things come to an end,' he said cheerfully.

From behind the wall a voice squeaked, 'Will someone let me out?'

The Doctor chuckled. 'Well, well, well, a mouse in the wainscotting. Well squeaked, mouse!'

He took out his sonic screwdriver and began to unscrew the wall-panel.

A short time later, Leela stood in the ore separation section watching the Doctor unlock the door of the TARDIS. 'Doctor, shouldn't we stay and make sure that Toos and Uvanov are all right?'

'No!' said the Doctor firmly. 'They've sent up their distress satellite, a rescue ship's on its way, and it's time we were on ours.' He threw open the TARDIS's door and waved Leela inside.

She paused in the doorway. 'Doctor, why didn't the helium make *your* voice squeaky?'

The Doctor smiled. 'Because I'm a Time Lord. I've been around, you know. Two hearts, a respiratory bypass system, and a larynx that will stand up to anything. I haven't lived seven hundred and fifty years without learning something. After you—mouse!'

Leela gave him a scornful look and stalked inside the TARDIS. The Doctor followed her, closing the door behind them.

With a wheezing, groaning sound, the blue box faded into nothingness.

The Doctor and Leela were on their way to new adventures.

TARGET STORY BOOKS

'Doctor Who'

0426

Terrance Dicks			
200098	**DOCTOR WHO AND THE HORROR OF FANG ROCK**		**60p**
Brian Hayles			
108663	**DOCTOR WHO AND THE ICE WARRIORS**		**60p**
Terrance Dicks			
110412	**DOCTOR WHO AND THE LOCH NESS MONSTER**		**60p**
Philip Hinchcliffe			
118936	**DOCTOR WHO AND THE MASQUE OF MANDRAGORA**		**60p**
Terrance Dicks			
116909	**DOCTOR WHO AND THE MUTANTS**		**60p**
Terrance Dicks			
116828	**DOCTOR WHO AND THE PLANET OF EVIL**		**60p**
Terrance Dicks			
116666	**DOCTOR WHO AND THE PYRAMIDS OF MARS**		**60p**
Malcolm Hulke			
11308X	**DOCTOR WHO AND THE SEA-DEVILS**	(illus)	**40p**
Philip Hinchcliffe			
116585	**DOCTOR WHO AND THE SEEDS OF DOOM**		**50p**
Malcolm Hulke			
110331	**DOCTOR WHO AND THE SPACE WAR**		**60p**
Terrance Dicks			
119738	**DOCTOR WHO AND THE TALONS OF WENG–CHIANG**		**60p**
Terrance Dicks			
110846	**DOCTOR WHO AND THE WEB OF FEAR**		**60p**
Bill Strutton			
113241	**DOCTOR WHO AND THE ZARBI**	(illus)	**60p**
Terrance Dicks			
114477	**THE DOCTOR WHO MONSTER BOOK**	(illus)	**50p**
200012	**THE SECOND DOCTOR WHO MONSTER BOOK**	(Colour illus)	**70p**
Terrance Dicks			
118421	**THE DOCTOR WHO DINOSAUR BOOK**		**75p**
116151	Terrance Dicks and Malcolm Hulke **THE MAKING OF DOCTOR WHO**	·	**60p**

† For sale in Britain and Ireland only.
*Not for sale in Canada.
♦ Film & T.V. tie-ins

TARGET STORY BOOKS

'Doctor Who'

200020	DOCTOR WHO DISCOVERS PREHISTORIC ANIMALS	(NF)	(illus)	75p
200039	DOCTOR WHO DISCOVERS SPACE TRAVEL	(NF)	(illus)	75p
200047	DOCTOR WHO DISCOVERS STRANGE AND MYSTERIOUS CREATURES	(NF)	(illus)	75p
20008X	DOCTOR WHO DISCOVERS THE STORY OF EARLY MAN	(NF)	(illus)	75p
200136	DOCTOR WHO DISCOVERS THE CONQUERORS	(NF)	(illus)	75p

Ian Marter
116313 DOCTOR WHO AND THE ARK IN SPACE 50p

Terrance Dicks
116747 DOCTOR WHO AND THE BRAIN OF MORBIUS 50p*

Terrance Dicks
110250 DOCTOR WHO AND THE CARNIVAL OF MONSTERS 50p

Malcolm Hulke
11471X DOCTOR WHO AND THE CAVE MONSTERS 60p

Terrance Dicks
117034 DOCTOR WHO AND THE CLAWS OF AXOS 50p*

David Whitaker
113160 DOCTOR WHO AND THE CRUSADERS (illus) 60p

Brian Hayles
114981 DOCTOR WHO AND THE CURSE OF PELADON 60p

Gerry Davis
114639 DOCTOR WHO AND THE CYBERMEN 60p

Barry Letts
113322 DOCTOR WHO AND THE DAEMONS (illus) 40p

David Whitaker
101103 DOCTOR WHO AND THE DALEKS 60p

Terrance Dicks
11244X DOCTOR WHO AND THE DALEK INVASION OF EARTH 60p

Terrance Dicks
119657 DOCTOR WHO AND THE DEADLY ASSASSIN 60p

Terrance Dicks
200063 DOCTOR WHO AND THE FACE OF EVIL 60p

Terrance Dicks
112601 DOCTOR WHO AND THE GENESIS OF THE DALEKS 60p

TARGET STORY BOOKS

Fantasy And General Fiction

		Elisabeth Beresford		
	101537	**AWKWARD MAGIC**	(illus)	60p
	10479X	**SEA-GREEN MAGIC**	(illus)	60p
	101618	**TRAVELLING MAGIC**	(illus)	60p
	119142	Eileen Dunlop **ROBINSHEUGH**	(illus)	60p
	112288	Maria Gripe **THE GLASSBLOWER'S CHILDREN**	(illus)	45p
	117891	Joyce Nicholson **FREEDOM FOR PRISCILLA**		70p
	106989	Hilary Seton **THE HUMBLES**	(illus)	50p
	109112	**THE NOEL STREATFEILD CHRISTMAS HOLIDAY BOOK**	(illus)	60p
	109031	**THE NOEL STREATFEILD EASTER HOLIDAY BOOK**	(illus)	60p
	105249	**THE NOEL STREATFEILD SUMMER HOLIDAY BOOK**	(illus)	50p

Humour

		Eleanor Estes		
	107519	**THE WITCH FAMILY**	(illus)	50p
	11762X	Felice Holman **THE WITCH ON THE CORNER**	(illus)	50p
	105672	Spike Milligan **BADJELLY THE WITCH**	(illus)	60p
	109546	**DIP THE PUPPY**	(illus)	60p
	107438	Christine Nostlinger **THE CUCUMBER KING**	(illus)	45p
	119223	Mary Rogers **A BILLION FOR BORIS**		60p

0426   Film And TV Tie-ins

		Kathleen N. Daly		
	200187	**RAGGEDY ANN AND ANDY** (Colour illus)		75p ♦ *
	11826X	John Ryder Hall **SINBAD AND THE EYE OF THE TIGER**		70p* ♦
	11535X	John Lucarotti **OPERATION PATCH**		45p
	119495	Pat Sandys **THE PAPER LADS**		60p ♦
	115511	Alison Thomas **BENJI**		40p

† For sale in Britain and Ireland only.
*Not for sale in Canada.
♦ Film & T.V. tie-ins

Wyndham Books are obtainable from many booksellers and newsagents. If you have any difficulty please send purchase price plus postage on the scale below to:

Wyndham Cash Sales
P.O. Box 11
Falmouth
Cornwall

While every effort is made to keep prices low, it is sometimes necessary to increase prices at short notice. Wyndham Books reserve the right to show new retail prices on covers which may differ from those advertised in the text or elsewhere.

Postage and Packing Rate

UK: 22p for the first book, plus 10p per copy for each additional book ordered to a maximum charge of 82p. **BFPO and Eire:** 22p for the first book, plus 10p per copy for the next 6 books and thereafter 4p per book. **Overseas:** 30p for the first book and 10p per copy for each additional book.

These charges are subject to Post Office charge fluctuations.